JUST BREATHIN' HATE

When the Law went loco and charged him with killing his wife, innocent Jack Fallon had two choices only — run or hang. So he ran — to a strange lost valley shut off from the world and ruled by a cult of holy men who would prove more lethal than any posse could ever be . . .

DEMPSEY CLAY

◆

JUST BREATHIN' HATE

Complete and Unabridged

LINFORD
Leicester

First published in Great Britain in 2008 by
Robert Hale Limited
London

First Linford Edition
published 2010
by arrangement with
Robert Hale Limited
London

British Library CIP Data

Clay, Dempsey.
    Just breathin' hate. - -
    (Linford western library)
    1. Western stories.
    2. Large type books.
    I. Title II. Series
    823.9'2–dc22

    ISBN 978–1–44480–128–6

Published by
F. A. Thorpe (Publishing)
Anstey, Leicestershire

Set by Words & Graphics Ltd.
Anstey, Leicestershire
Printed and bound in Great Britain by
T. J. International Ltd., Padstow, Cornwall

This book is printed on acid-free paper

1

Get Fallon

They were gaining now. He could hear the shouts of men and the baying of hounds in the distance. Yet it was hard to tell just how close they might be that storm-tossed September day. Gusts of wind shook the heavy oaks and brought acorns rattling down as the rider moved out from beneath the trees and warily started across a natural clearing.

Somewhere behind, somewhere on the timbered slopes of this unfamiliar mountain, horsemen armed with rifles and wearing badges were following him relentlessly.

A jagged fork of lightning slammed into a nearby hillside. By its hellish blue light the hunted man glimpsed a track leading upwards from the clearing, and reeled towards it. A husky man with dark hair plastered to his face by the drenching rain and blue eyes sunken with pain and mounting exhaustion, he was almost at the end of his tether.

But now night was coming down.

If he could just get to stay ahead of them until dark he might stand a chance.

Low-hanging limbs sought to slow his progress and his worn boots slipped on the wet grass. He was climbing steeply by this time and the breath rasped painfully in his throat. His legs were leaden. The impulse to quit grew stronger as he kicked and clawed his way along a seemingly endless animal path which twisted its way through the woods. Simply to give in and let them catch him was a temptation he was finding harder and harder to resist every mile.

Why not let St George take you? whispered a treacherous inner voice. Let St George sling another hang rope around his neck and finish what he'd failed to finish back in San Pedro.

Back in San Pedro . . .

Jack Fallon's eyes clouded with violent memories as his hand went to his neck again to trace the vicious rope scar there with his fingertips. Once again he was sitting his saddle beneath San Pedro's hanging tree with the heavy noose tight about his neck. He stared down at the blur of faces and heard St George's deep voice announcing why he had been condemned to death.

Then came the cut of the quirt across the horse's rump, the sickening plunge forward and the fierce bite of the rope into his flesh — followed by the rifle-like report as the limb of the hanging tree broke.

The limb had been sawn almost completely through!

Fallon saw this with disbelieving eyes even as the frightened horse bore him away with the trailing yellow rope flying behind.

Somebody wanted him to live!

Ripping the noose free from his neck and raking with both heels, he booted the frightened horse furiously into the dim grey light of the early morning mist.

They came after him like howling Comanches — but didn't catch him. Not in the first mile or the next fifty as the pursuers dropped further and further behind with every mile and cursed bitterly that a lowly sheepman could own such a wonderful horse.

That horse was dead now. Fallon was forced to shoot it when it broke its leg in a gopher hole after he'd lost the posse. And right now he was thinking of quitting in a way that fine animal had never done . . .

The thought fired up his strength.

He lifted his chin and sucked air into tortured lungs. Gradually but surely his stride lengthened. He realized darkness had fallen over the landscape while he'd been reliving his nightmares. The trees had given away to giant boulders and now there was a roaring sound in his ears that rose above the endless beat of the rain.

'Fallon, you bastard!' he heard a remote voice shout, and recognized the unmistakable voice of Marshal Rogan St George.

Although no longer able to see where he was going, sheer determination and the instinct for survival kept him relentlessly placing one weary foot after another — until that moment when he lost his footing and found himself tumbling helplessly in the grip of a raging mountain torrent.

He had mere seconds to realize he'd stumbled into a river before he was borne over the lip of the waterfall.

He scrabbled wildly with both hands but there was nothing to grip. He was plummeting straight downwards in a cascade of icy water with the name of his murdered wife on his lips when his head glanced off a rock and blackness engulfed him.

* * *

The Brethren welcomed each new day with a prayer.

The morning assembly was usually held in the big stone church in Trinity. Yet because it was such a beautiful morning and everybody seemed so pleased to see the sun again after a week of bad weather, Deacon Brown conducted the prayers out on the broad landing in front of the feed barn.

Nobody skipped prayers in Resurrection Valley.

Here, deep in the Roblais Mountains, it was considered more important to pray than to eat, and more desirable to die young in the state of grace than live to one hundred as a sinner.

The deacon said so and his pronouncements on matters of faith were rarely questioned.

'Let us give thanks that the great storms have passed without loss of life amongst the Brethren!' he boomed, robed arms stretching heavenwards. 'And let us beseech Thee now for a spell of clement weather to enable us to complete our sowing chores before winter sets in.'

6

Rotund Deacon Brown, sixty, bald and vigorous, was a man with both a spiritual and a practical side to his nature. He wasn't shy about asking God for something to make life easier, such as fine weather or a rise in crop prices. He was an intelligent, God-fearing man who led his people with wisdom and strength in Resurrection Valley, yet was regarded with deep mistrust and hostility by the world outside.

'Immoralist,' was one of the gentler slurs reserved for Deacon Brown in the valley lands east of the mountains and in the town of Woodstock. 'Servant of Satan', 'Harem Man' and 'Antichrist' were others.

Yet had the deacon been vulnerable to the criticism of the Outsiders he would surely never have chosen to live as he did.

This man prayed for his detractors, turned the other cheek to his enemies and blessed all those who wished to hurl the Brethren out of the valley and

7

burn down everything they had built here.

But on this brighter morning all that interested him was the weather.

'I ask you,' he exhorted the kneeling Brethren, 'to join with me in silent prayer entreating the Lord to send us a batch of pretty weather for at least a couple of weeks. Then He can let the heavens and floodwaters roar — or whatever He pleases.'

It was magnanimous of the deacon to permit heaven to send down some foul weather at a later date. But whether due to the leader's prayers or simply because the wind had blown all the rain away, the morning remained fine and golden — and as such proved too much temptation to Francine and Rebecca.

When the girls saddled their ponies they told Matthew they were going berry-picking, and carried wicker baskets to support the story. This was a lie, and they'd been taught there was no such thing as a white lie; all lies were as black as the devil's bootstraps when tested by the valley's rigid codes.

This worried Francine as they went loping across the wide valley with the wind in their hair, yet didn't concern her friend in the least.

'A day like this comes along only a few times every year, Francie,' Rebecca exulted as they cantered along the banks of a deep irrigation ditch. 'It would surely be a sin not to enjoy it.'

Francine, as dark as her companion was golden blonde, considered that a moment then finally nodded in agreement.

'Well, if we are going to enjoy it, Becky,' she cried, leaning over her horse's neck, 'let's do it properly.' She raised her quirt. 'Race you to the High Chapel!'

She was off like a shot, her mount's hoofs throwing up clods of damp earth, hair, dress and scarf all billowing behind her as she reached full gallop.

'You stole the start!' Becky laughed accusingly, then used hands and heels to lift her mount to full pace and went racing after her.

The high valley, cupped and protected here by the arms of the mighty mountains, was a magnificent sight. Shaped like a flat iron with the broad northern end butting against the brooding cliffs of Black Range and the opposite and narrow end five miles due south, Resurrection Valley was a place of timeless stone, sweeping vistas and dreaming peaks. Green meadows splashed by sunlight flowed away into the darker regions of the forests which climbed steeply on all sides in a series of rugged cliffs.

The Brethren produced virtually all they needed in the valley. The climate and soil were suitable for both farming and cattle-raising. There were sheep, goats, alfalfa fields and wheat. There was no sound reason why any settler should fail in this lush valley unless he was lazy.

Becky was gradually overtaking Francine as they raced over a series of undulating hills. Perched upon higher ground ahead and outlined sharply against the sombre backdrop of the Black Range cliff, stood the High Chapel.

The small stone chapel had been the first place of worship erected by the deacon and his followers upon their arrival in the valley several years earlier.

It was still used as a place of retreat and pilgrimage by the Brethren, although it was anything but spiritual need which brought the girls there today. They simply wanted to get away — away from all the piety and the responsibility of simply being good twenty-four hours a day.

They certainly were not bad, but nor were they as sinless — as defined by the Brethren — as they might have been, either.

Whenever they could escape like this they enjoyed racing their ponies in a way their elders would have regarded as tomboyish, then hitched up their skirts to go paddling and frolicking in the Holy Water River.

They also got to exchange confidences,

11

gossiped without restriction and in general behaved like a couple of normal, high-spirited young women anywhere.

The race was virtually a draw.

Panting and laughing they unsaddled the horses, put them on tethers, then strolled around the chapel chewing blades of grass and soaking up the sunshine.

Becky threw her arms at the sky.

'I wish I could fly, Francie. Wouldn't you simply love to fly off up into that blue sky and keep going until you came to the very best place in all the world? Wouldn't you?'

Francine sometimes took her friend too literally and seriously. 'But surely this is the best place in the world, isn't it?'

Becky smiled impishly. 'We don't know that, do we? We're not allowed to see anything or do anything other than what is to be found here. I'd surely love to see what's out there beyond crummy old Woodstock town so I could judge what is good or bad for myself instead of simply being told.'

Francine frowned.

'I don't think you should be speaking that way, Becky. I'm sure the elders wouldn't like it.'

'Oh, pshaw! Those old fuddy-duddies don't really like anything but praying and dying!'

'Becky!'

'All right. I suppose I should not be disrespectful. Come on, let's paddle.'

Sunlight sparkled upon Holy Water River. Even in the shallows they could feel the strength of the current. With skirts tucked up and the sun in their faces they waded along like children, giggling and laughing at anything at all, until Francine mentioned Carver Brown.

Immediately Becky's pert face shadowed.

'I'd rather not speak of Carver today, Francie.'

'All right, honey. I just thought you might be interested to know what he said about you . . . '

Becky waded to the bank and sat in the sand letting the sun dry her legs.

She did not want to appear curious, and yet she was.

'So . . . what did he say?' she asked at last.

Francine came and sat beside her.

'Carver said you are the prettiest girl either in or out of the valley.'

Becky looked away sharply. Being a normal twenty-year-old she enjoyed compliments. But not from Carver Brown. The deacon's eldest son disturbed her deeply. She had always found him arrogant and vaguely threatening, more so in recent times than ever before, so it seemed. About the only thing Carver had in his favour, in her eyes, was that he was young.

And Deacon Brown was so old . . .

Her eyes filled with tears. Deacon Brown planned to marry her very shortly. He already had two wives, but polygamy was permitted amongst the Brethren. This was the principal reason the clan was so intensely disliked and mistrusted beyond the valleys by the 'Outsiders.'

Becky had romantic dreams of a monogamous union, yet Deacon Brown had already set the date for their wedding, and it was imminent.

'Why don't you like Carver, Becky?' Francine considered Carver Brown a fine catch — rugged, handsome, virile and respected. She wished he would talk about how beautiful *she* was.

'I feel like walking,' Becky said sharply, jumping to her feet and making off upstream. 'You don't have to come if you don't want . . .'

It wasn't much of an invitation but Francine went along anyway. They were soon out of sight of the chapel, walking barefoot along a grassy bank under graceful willows where Becky's natural good spirits quickly revived.

When they finally tired they sat down side-by-side amongst a cluster of large, water-weathered boulders and indulged in their favourite pastime. They talked about the kind of Prince Charming each would like to meet one day, where and how they might live, the children and fine times they would get to enjoy.

The sun had reached its zenith and the stream sparkled and gurgled as it went rushing on by. Admiring her small naked feet under the water, Becky allowed her gaze to drift upstream, then suddenly stiffened.

She found herself staring at another foot, this one encased in a sodden leather boot and protruding from between two rocks.

Instantly she jumped to her feet so sharply that her companion turned in her direction, and she too saw the imprisoned foot. They traded fearful glances. Francine, now on her feet, was tempted to run, but Becky seized her arm and held her tightly.

'No, we can't just go. We'll have to see who it is, Francie.'

Francine's dark eyes stretched even wider. 'But . . . but surely it could only be an Outsider!'

'Outsider' was an ugly word in the high valley. It meant alien, hostile and dangerous, and applied to anyone from beyond the limits of the great valley.

'I don't care who it is,' Becky said determinedly, dragging her companion along with her. 'Come on!'

Both halted sharply when they leaned over the shielding boulders. The man lay on his back, wedged between rocks. He was either unconscious or dead and it seemed by merest chance that he'd come to rest with his head and torso held up out of the water by rocks.

'My God, Becky. It is an Outsider! Is he . . . is he . . . ?'

'Dead?'

The word chilled Becky. For this man was young and strongly-built with a fine open face and manly features. It seemed tragic for anybody to perish all alone and in such a manner and her heart went out to him, whoever he might be.

Then Francine gasped. The dead man's chest had just moved. He was still breathing!

2

Marshal of San Pedro

They rode into Woodstock around noon, twelve trail-stained possemen on tired horses. The whole bunch reeked of disappointment. Unshaven faces, red eyes and sullen silence proclaimed this as they dismounted at the long hitchrails outside the Frontier Saloon.

The porch sitters and bar room loafers of Woodstock weren't left long to speculate upon the reason behind the new arrivals' moodiness, for once they had downed their first shots the possemen of San Pedro proved anything but reticent.

They had pursued a convicted murderer up into the Roblais Mountains then lost him, they revealed. Who wouldn't feel feel peeved by something like that?

'Hell, it'd be easy enough to lose a hundred hellions up in them mountains, gents,' proclaimed saloon-keeper Darby Wilkes. A big man with a vast belly, Wilkes was also mayor of the community and an expert on the local terrain. He shrugged. 'So, don't feel bad about losing one geezer.'

'What if we want to feel bad about it, mister?'

The speaker was the posse captain, a large, rawboned man wearing a lawman's badge pinned to a sleeveless leather vest.

Darby Wilkes sized him up with shrewd eyes. 'You'd be St George, I take it?'

'Marshal St George, that is.'

Wilkes cocked an eyebrow. 'You the one that let this here murderer get away on you then . . . Marshal?'

St George bristled. He was a hard man and looked it every inch. Yet portly Wilkes wasn't intimidated. He was one of the biggest men in this tough town, with plenty of friends, several of whom were present at the moment. Two of these made their deliberate way across to the bar then leaned upon their elbows and stared the marshal of San Pedro squarely in the eye.

'I'm not sure I like your tone, mister,' St George stated, unintimidated.

'If it comes right down to cases, I don't much admire yours,' countered Wilkes.

'Oh, hell, take it easy, gents,' growled a barrel-bellied posseman. He grinned at Wilkes. 'We're all kind of worn thin and played out, Darby. Two days without proper sleep or hot chow . . . you understand?'

'Sure, Judd,' said Wilkes, subjecting the formidable marshal to a closer scrutiny. 'Who'd this feller murder anyway?'

'His wife.'

A percentage girl stifled a shocked sound and even tough Darby Wilkes shook his head grimly.

'A wife-killer! I guess that's about as low as any man can get.' He inhaled and looked questioningly at the posse-men. 'So, how come he escaped?'

Judd Venner related the story of the hanging tree and the sawn limb. While he spoke Marshal St George stood with a shot glass in a big fist staring off at nothing, jaw muscles working.

'Who sawed that there tree?' a barfly was curious to know.

'We'll find that out in time,' St George interjected. 'After we catch Fallon.'

'Fallon?' echoed Joe Cosgrove of Woodstock's bank. 'Is that this fugitive's name?'

'John Joseph Fallon, known as Jack, late of Comstock Ranch,' supplied a brooding St George. 'Five feet ten inches tall, weight one-eighty, hair and eyes dark, regular features.'

He paused to grimace as if tasting something bitter, then added:

'Convicted killer and escapee from lawful custody. Execution pending.'

He might have been quoting word for word from a wanted dodger. 'No, there's no reward for catching this man other than the satisfaction of bringing to justice one of the lowest breeds known to mankind.'

'Haven't sighted anybody answering that description around Woodstock,' stated Wilkes.

'Of course you haven't,' snapped St George. 'Because he'd be up in the high country.'

Wilkes flushed, offended. But St George ignored him as he swung to face his men. 'And just in case any of you are in any doubt we're gonna run Fallon down if we have to cover every square inch of this lousy country.'

This drew groans of weary protest. All had businesses to get back to, families to care for. Some were saddle sore and others had developed crippling head colds. They'd had their fill of manhunting, but their leader plainly had not.

'Dawn!' St George reiterated, turning to leave. 'And any posseman who fails to present himself before the hotel at the appointed hour will have me to reckon with — personally!'

With a curt nod he was gone, his rawboned frame filling the doorway before he disappeared.

'Whew!' said bearded Bradley of the Woodstock Stage Company. 'He's sure set on running down this Fallon pilgrim, ain't he?'

'He seems to be taking the whole thing personal,' observed Wilkes.

'And I reckon he does at that,' conceded posseman Judd Venner. 'But like always, the marshal has his reasons.'

'What are they?' asked Wilkes.

The posseman lowered his glass and met each man's eyes in turn before responding in a low but clear voice that carried.

'At his trial, Fallon swore he didn't murder his wife. He claimed the marshal done it!'

★ ★ ★

There was a sensation of rising weightlessly upwards from a darkness which now grew slowly lighter and lighter until suddenly his eyes snapped open.

He expected to find himself in water — it was the last thing he remembered before blacking out. Instead he seemed to be free-floating before a ghostly figure clad all in white with hands oustretched before him, her dim face filled with tender sorrow.

An angel!

He must have drowned and gone to heaven!

There followed a drifting lurch in time that might have been an hour or merely a moment before he felt a cool hand on his forehead.

'It's all right,' said the voice — it could only be an angel. 'You are going to be fine.'

With a fierce act of will Fallon shook his upper body then rose onto one elbow. The world lurched crazily for a moment and in the next he saw that the angel was in reality a flesh and blood woman. That mysterious glow that had surrounded her head and shoulders was simply sunlight pouring down through a stained glass window.

He blinked and realized he was in some kind of church.

His stomach heaved alarmingly and he tasted river water. Instantly, a second girl appeared and held a battered pail beneath his jaws. Fallon put his head over it and threw up what felt like a gallon of river water.

He slumped back weakly on the makeshift couch that had been fashioned by placing several pews together. The blonde girl placed a cold compress on his brow and in mere moments he was seeing and thinking almost as clearly as ever.

'Do you feel better now?'

He nodded then stretched. He realized that apart from a nagging pain in his right ankle he was feeling virtually normal.

But how come?

Last thing he recalled was going under the river waters for the last time . . .

He blinked and realized the girl was smiling. She was pretty; that was the first thing he noticed. Snubnosed and bright-eyed she wore a homespun blue robe gathered at the waist by a rope cord. The second girl standing at her shoulder was contrastingly dark-haired and wide-eyed but dressed in the same fashion. They seemed puzzled by his presence and maybe just a little alarmed to find him here — wherever in hell that might be.

'How'd I get here?' he breathed.

'We found you in the Holy Water River,' replied the blonde. 'Mr Fallon.'

'Fallon?'

'That is your name, isn't it?' The dark girl held his Colt up for him to see. His name was inscribed in copperplate etching upon the butt.

He drew himself up into a more comfortable position. 'Who are you . . . and just where am I?'

They supplied their names and related how they'd found him half drowned in the river before employing a sled and mule to haul him up to the chapel close by.

'I suspect we may have stumbled upon you just in time, Mr Fallon,' smiled the blonde girl. 'I'm Rebecca and this is Francine.' She grimaced. 'We really thought you were dead.'

'Better call me Jack seeing as you saved my life.' He tried to smile but couldn't quite make it. 'Your folks ranchers hereabouts?'

'Well, I suppose you'd call them ranchers with a difference,' dark-haired Francine supplied. She folded her hands in her lap and nodded. 'We are really religious folk first and farmers and cattle ranchers second.'

'Well all I can say is I'm mighty grateful. You live hereabouts?'

'We belong to the Brethren,' Rebecca stated. 'The Brethren of Resurrection Valley.'

Fallon looked blank. Francine nodded

to Rebecca. 'It seems obvious he's never heard of us, Becky. Well what are we going to do with him now?'

Fallon's gaze flicked from one to the other as he mused; Did they know? Had word circulated that an escaped killer was in the region? Were their menfolk close by? Maybe the posse?

It seemed a long silent moment before Rebecca answered. And it was not the answer he expected.

'We'll simply have to hide him until he's well enough to travel, Francie.'

'But what if they should find out?' Francine cried in alarm.

'If who finds out?' Fallon wanted to know.

Rebecca placed a calming hand on his shoulder.

'The Brethren never allow Outsiders into the valley uninvited, Mr Fallon. The Outsiders don't trust us and we certainly do not trust them. If an Outsider is ever sighted in our regions we are obliged to report it to the deacon immediately, and then allow the menfolk to take care of the matter.'

Fallon swallowed.

'Take care . . . ?' he queried.

'There's no love lost between the Brethren and the Outsiders, Mr Fallon,' Francine explained. 'Indeed some interlopers here have been treated very harshly by Carver and his men over time. We do not wish to see that happen to you.'

'That makes three of us then,' Fallon said soberly, swinging his feet to the floor. 'But you don't have to worry any about me, girls. I can make it — '

The moment he stood his right ankle gave way. He fell against a pew, knocking it over. The girls helped him get seated again. The ankle was sending jolts of pain up his leg into the hip.

'You've either sprained that ankle or broken it,' Rebecca said calmly. 'Either way, you can't walk.'

'I could ride,' he insisted.

'You'd never get past the lookouts,' Francine insisted.

'They can't have sentries all over this

damned valley,' Fallon protested. He was, of course, deeply grateful, yet stubbornness and independence were beginning to raise their heads now. He wanted to get moving before there was a knock on the door and twenty rifle-toting holy-rollers burst in.

'We don't need lookouts all over,' Rebecca pointed out calmly. 'Only down at the mouth of the valley, which is the the only entrance and exit.'

Standing at the window she gestured at the encircling ironstone cliffs, lofty and forbidding. 'You see?'

It was some time before Fallon nodded. 'All right,' he grunted. 'But it's plain I can't hole up here on account it would be too risky for you girls, as I see it. And I'm getting the clear notion that your menfolk here play the game hard and by their own rules . . . '

His words trailed off as he realized Francine was looking at his neck. He glanced down. His collar was opened and the rope scar on his neck was clearly visible.

'What happened to your neck, Mr Fallon?' she wanted to know.

'My necktie got too tight.'

He knew he spoke harshly. He couldn't help it. The horror of his near hanging was still too fresh and vivid.

The girls withdrew to the doorway to talk in low tones. Fallon made another attempt to stand but was forced to give it best. He watched his rescuers. They appeared to be arguing now. He sensed Rebecca wanted him to remain in the chapel while Francine argued they should either get him out of this building or else report his presence to the Brethren. The girl sounded scared. He sensed she might have good reason to be so.

Rebecca finally won, and considering the way his injury felt, he was damned glad she did.

They left him a blanket, a little food and a canteen of water. Rebecca promised to return some time during the night with other things he might need, including something for the pain.

31

She warned him to keep to the chapel and not show himself. If anybody should come he was to hide in the vestry. Did he have any questions before they left?

Only one. 'Can I have my six-gun back?'

This touched off another debate, but again Rebecca prevailed and Francine returned the weapon to him, albeit warily.

Fallon hefted his piece thoughtfully. He was no gunhand yet felt far better with the weapon in his hand again than without it. Instinct warned this was dangerous country. He glanced up from the Colt to meet their questioning eyes.

'I won't use it unless I have to, girls,' he promised. When he sensed they needed more reassurance, he added, 'All right. I swear not to use it unless my life is in danger. How's that?'

They nodded and left a short time later. He listened to the hoofbeats fading away down the slopes. He was left with St Peter and the Colt .45. Plus his thoughts, of course. Right now, fugitive Jack Fallon had enough of those to occupy his mind fully and then some.

3

The Violent Men

Warmed by the late afternoon light streaming through his study window, Deacon Brown, rugged and ruddy-faced in his sober black cassock, was putting the finishing touches to his Sunday sermon.

As usual he was well pleased with the finished article, and reread the page with some pride.

He liked to compare composing a sermon to baking a cake. It required a generous amount of brotherly love, a pinch or two of charity, and in equal parts, dobs of faith, hope and honour for your father and mother topped off by a stern measure of warning against coveting thy neighbour's wife.

The good deacon never dwelt too long on the contentious topic of lust, due to the fact that lust and Deacon Brown were not exactly strangers.

For despite already boasting two wives, the man of the cloth was now finalizing the procedure necessary to take unto himself a third. The most charitable explanation for this intention would appear to be lust.

The deacon paused for a moment to suck on the end of his quill pen and reflect upon Sister Rebecca and the way her slim hips moved beneath her blue robe as she walked.

He shook his head and turned his attention to the window.

Outside, all the Brethren who laboured in the service of the Lord in Resurrection Valley were bringing their day's tasks to a close.

The Deacon smiled benignly and mused: *my children*. Then, reminding himself they looked to him for spiritual guidance as well as temporal leadership, he returned to his sermon.

He nodded approvingly as he read it through. It was heavily laced with hellfire and damnation, surefire ingredients to make them sit up and take notice. He saw himself as a two-fisted man of the cloth unafraid to give it to the worshippers with both barrels whenever he thought they needed it.

A gentle tap sounded on the door.

'Come!' called the deacon and his plump second wife entered carrying a tray of coffee and sweet cakes.

He smiled at her fondly and gave her a little pat of approval as she left. But as the door closed on her back the deacon leaned back in his chair, sober and thoughtful.

The zing and zest appeared to be slipping from his life, he mused. He had a nagging feeling of disharmony threatening from all sides — disharmony and boredom. The hostility of the Outsiders towards them appeared to be strengthening every day, while he was no longer as close to his sons as he'd once been, Carver in particular.

He snorted and took a deep pull on his coffee. It was only too plain that he needed change and must secure it, he assured himself.

And what in this life could be more of a welcome change than a young new bride?

He was standing by his window hoping for a chance glimpse of Rebecca a short time later when Carver suddenly appeared in the doorway of his lodge across the way, which was second in size only to the deacon's own.

Although dressed in black like all his fellow Brethren, Carver Brown stood out from everyone else in this place. Tall and immensely powerful with a black spade beard and brooding eyes, the deacon's eldest son ranked as the most formidable man in Resurrection Valley.

Not everybody saw Carver in that light, yet his own father certainly did. The deacon knew that many of the Brethren believed they needed a two-fisted man of God to lead and guide them through the increasingly uncertain times ahead, and so regarded

Carver as that future leader.

It was subtly hinted occasionally that he should step down and give Carver his chance. But Deacon Brown wasn't ready to relinquish the leadership just yet, and in any case was far from convinced Carver was the right man to replace him.

The friction between father and son had become more evident since the deacon had announced his intentions to wed Rebecca Marsh, for many suspected Carver wanted the young beauty for himself.

Deacon Brown gusted a sigh as he watched his son stride down to the horse corrals like a man who never wearied.

The deacon often wished second son, Aaron, had more of Carver's vigour, or that his third son, Matthew, was less of a dreamer. Secretly, he believed either would make a better leader than Carver — when that time came.

Nonetheless the deacon would never deny that Carver was essential to the continued strength and security of all Brethren. On many occasions his big son had proven himself more than a match for their enemies on the outside — and was about to do so again.

Four horsemen were coming in via the east trail from the valley mouth, two Brethren sentries and two others. One man was the deputy sheriff of Woodstock, the other a massive stranger in a fringed buckskin jacket.

The deacon made his way outside and walked down to the gate where the horsemen reined in.

'Deputy Slater from Woodstock and Elwood Treece from San Pedro, Deacon,' called one of the sentries. 'They seek permission to search the valley.'

'Search the valley?' The deacon moved forward to halt by Carver's side. 'What on earth for?'

'We're looking for a fugitive,' grunted the sour-featured deputy. Slater let his gaze drift over the stronghold, then spat in the dust. 'A woman-killer they were fixing to hang over in San Pedro busted loose a few days back. Seems the marshal from down that way formed a posse and chased the killer into the Roblais Mountains but lost him in the storms. We reckon he might've headed for these parts, eh, Mr Treece?'

'Correct.'

Elwood Treece dismounted without asking permission. A giant of a man with a hectic red face and fierce eyes, he was lawman Rogan St George's right-hand man and a notorious brawler. He fixed a hard eye upon the deacon. 'You're the head man here, I take it?'

Brown lifted his clean shaven chin.

'I am Deacon Brown sir. And before I give permission for anything I must be in possession of all the facts. Now, what is this fugitive's name and crime?'

'Jack Fallon. And he murdered his wife!'

★   ★   ★

Step, stop, step, stop . . .

Fallon leaned upon his improvised

walking stick and sleeved sweat from his forehead. Although determined to fight his way back to fitness before he got tracked down and hauled back to San Pedro to hang, he had to admit he was making slow progress. The ankle still would not support his weight even though the swelling was receding and there was no sign of a bone break.

Sweat from his clumsy exertions stung his eyes as he stared upslope at the chapel. He cursed his lack of progress, dragged his sleeve across his face then started off again, determined to reach his objective without another rest no matter how much it hurt.

It hurt the very first step. He set it down more gingerly next time, and heard 'click!'

He cursed. What now?

The fence was close by. He decided to go sit on a low rail and examine the leg. He set the injured foot down gingerly — and felt nothing. He frowned in puzzlement. How come no real pain? What was going on? More

41

boldly, he took a forward step resting his entire weight on the affected limb to realize that apart from a fading soreness and the swelling, the ankle suddenly felt sound as a bell.

It seemed the click he'd heard was the sound of something vital slotting back into place.

Within minutes he was walking freely, which led to the only logical conclusion. The damage he'd sustained must have been a dislocation, not a break or strain as suspected, and in its own good time had readjusted itself.

He began to laugh out loud but quickly sobered as his gaze dropped to the town far below the slope. Sure, this was a lucky break, and he would make the most of it. But he was still a long way from escaping this vast and alien valley without even a horse to ride.

Then he remembered his pretty girls and sat down patiently to wait until they showed again to give them his good news.

And thought: despite losing the

woman he loved, standing trial, dodging the hangman by pure chance and surviving a manhunt and near drowning, he was suddenly feeling strong again, positive.

It felt like emerging from a long darkness.

He told himself his first priority would be simply to survive both the valley and the posse. The second would be to hunt down his wife's murderer, even if it took the rest of his life.

★ ★ ★

Following a thoughtful silence Deacon Brown nodded soberly then spoke up clearly.

'Upon consideration of your request, gentlemen, I regret my response must be in the negative. Licence to invade this valley is denied!'

Treece reddened. He spread heavy legs and hooked both thumbs in his wide leather belt. 'Why the hell not? You folks here against law and order like

43

everybody says?'

'This valley is God's garden, sir,' replied the deacon. 'No disbeliever is ever permitted to tarry here. Apart from that, your fugitive is not here.'

'How can you be sure?'

'I know everything that happens in my valley and there is no Outsider among us.' Brown paused, then added accusingly, 'Except for yourselves, gentlemen.'

'Told you it'd be a waste of time, Treece,' grumbled the deputy. 'They never let nobody in here nohow.'

Yet Elwood Treece was not so easily discouraged. The man was St George's loyal sidekick and it was the marshal who'd sent him here. He wouldn't let his superior down.

'You just don't seem to get the idea, Brown.' he said, heavy jaw jutting. 'We don't mean to let some bloody-handed killer slip through our fingers just because a bunch of damn harem men say we can't look wherever we want. You'd better think again about letting us check this here valley. It just could be we won't take no for an answer.'

'Sir!' a voice called. 'What is this fugitive's name?'

Treece's gaze sought out the speaker. It was pretty Rebecca March.

'Fallon,' he supplied. 'Jack Fallon.'

Carver Brown scowled as he jabbed a finger at the girl. 'You should know better than to horn in on men's matters, Becky,' he growled. He swung back to face the Outsiders, dropping a heavy hand on the deacon's arm as the man made to speak. 'I'll handle this, Deacon.'

'But — '

'I said I'll handle it!' Carver said loudly, and moved to confront Treece at close quarters. The San Pedro giant inflated his chest and slapped hands loudly against his shell belt in a warning gesture, yet Carver Brown was unmoved. 'Get!' he said loudly.

Treece blinked. 'What?'

'You just insulted us.'

'What? Oh, you mean calling you

harem men? Hell, that's what you are, ain't you. Or was I told wrong when I heard in Woodstock about your strange ways and how you Holy Joes can wed as many females as you please just like them there sheiks — '

'Get mounted and get gone!' Carver overrode him. 'I won't say it again.'

'And what'll you do if I don't? Pray for a thunderbolt from heaven to strike me down?'

Elwood Treece showed his appreciation of his own wit by slapping his big belly. He leaned back, laughing and showed all his yellowed teeth. 'Haw, haw, haw!'

Carver Brown's expression showed no change as he slammed his fist into the bigger man's jaw and felled him to the ground. Treece lay dazed a moment, unable to believe any holy joe could pack such a wallop. Then his head cleared and he sprang erect, raging.

'Why you psalm-singing scum!' he roared, and charged Carver with both arms flailing.

Brown did not give an inch. He was no boxer but was surely uncommonly strong with a natural capacity for violence. His technique was simple: he kept striking an adversary until he fell down. It was bad luck this also happened to be the same style favoured by this adversary.

Treece absorbed that fearful blow and struck back.

The brawl that ensued was something to see. Two men, one of them big and the other huge, tore into one another with a ferocity which would have seemed shocking any place and seemed doubly so in a place of peace and brotherly love.

Until Carver finally battered his way through his opponent's defences to deliver his Sunday punch — a short explosive right hook to the jaw.

Treece staggered, spitting blood and seeing stars. Instinct saw him raise his arms protectively as Carver came after him. Carver switched his attack to the belly to draw the arms down, then whipped an elbow into his face. Treece roared and swung a haymaker that missed by a mile and his momentum carried him straight into the right hook to the jaw that followed a split-second later.

Treece was down on one knee, spitting blood. He was up again but Carver was all over him, hitting and hurting, his eyes glittering with savage pleasure.

'All right, enough's enough!' bawled a pale-faced deputy. 'Back up, Carver, you'll kill the man!'

Aaron and Matthew rushed in to seize Carver by the arms, and only then did he shrug and permit his brothers to drag him away. He left his adversary on the ground on all fours, coughing crimson. The deacon rapped out orders and onlookers hurried to lift Treece off the ground and load him onto his horse.

'Now get the hell out of our valley and don't come back!' Carver Brown ordered.

'The marshal ain't gonna like this,' Slater warned as he started off, leading Treece's horse. 'And he can be a mighty ornery man when he has to be.'

'Get!' one of the elders barked and Deputy Slater got fast.

The Brethren were still excited as they gathered about the Brown brothers at the water trough. Aaron swabbed the blood from Carver's face while Matthew ripped away a section of his cassock which had been torn to pieces in the mêlée. Carver's bare chest heaved. His beard glistened with sweat and his black eyes were still filled with fire as he accepted the accolades.

'They'll think twice before they come again,' he predicted, still panting. 'The only way Outsiders will ever leave us be is by knowing who's stronger.' He spat and sleeved his mouth, frowning challengingly when he saw his father shouldering his way through the crowd. 'Right, old man?'

'You acted with courage and fortitude, my son. Yet I believe the same result could have been achieved by more peaceful means.'

Carver sneered. 'Fortune favours the brave, Father.'

The deacon frowned. 'I do not know that quotation, my son. Deuteronomy?'

'Virgil.'

'Oh.'

The deacon's sole source of inspiration was the Holy Bible. He had no time for poets, heathen poets least of all. His face hardened as he said, 'In future we shall solve our problems by the ways of peace and light, Carver, not by blood and anger. Is that understood?'

Carver shrugged his brothers away. This was not just another of an endless succession of clashes between father and son, he sensed. This was a confrontation.

'They hate us,' Carver declared, hands on hips. 'All Outsiders hate us because they don't understand our ways and because we won't conform to theirs. And they will grind us down and run us out of our valley if we give them half a chance, but not if they fear us. It's time we showed more strength and resolve, old man. If we wish to go on surviving we must regard the Outsiders as our mortal enemies and be prepared to deal with them as such. I respect the Book as well as you but unlike you I do not believe the Bible alone is powerful enough to protect us. Unless every man of us is prepared to fight with strength of purpose then that Book is just so many sheafs of paper!'

The deacon was shocked. 'Blasphemy!'

'Common sense!' Carver countered.

'My son, I fear for your soul.'

'Old man, I fear for our people!'

The deacon paused to study the faces about him. They appeared respectful of him as always. Yet there was another element present today which he noted and identified. Agreement with Carver. They had seen the intruder challenged and whipped and it had excited them. That was written plainly upon every face, so plainly in fact that suddenly

Deacon Brown felt like an old and weary man in the company of his husky son.

With a slow gesture he simply turned and moved through the silent bunch, pausing only for a word with Rebecca. He then headed off up the slope for his house where he intended getting down on his knees to pray for both his son and his flock.

Appearing suddenly larger in the eyes of the others now, Carver Brown watched his father out of sight before shouldering his way through the dark-garbed throng to reach Rebecca's side.

'He's old,' he said in a deep voice. 'He has an old man's shortness of breath and an old man's timidity.'

'You should not speak of your father that way, Brother Carver,' she chided. 'It is against the laws.'

'The time to keep the truth at bay is past. The Brethren now look to me for truth and leadership, as you must yourself, Sister Rebecca.'

'Respect is earned, not commanded.'

The man leaned closer and spoke softly so only she could hear.

'You shall never wed him!' he hissed. He seized her wrist, emotion working powerful features. 'The truth is you need a stallion not a bleating old he-goat!'

She made to pull away but he was too strong.

'You'll be my bride and we'll rule the valley between us. You know it, I know it, and the old man is the only one who doesn't.'

She finally succeeded in pulling free of his grasp but in doing so dropped the satchel she was carrying, disgorging its contents. She hastily gathered up her things and hurried away, leaving Carver watching her with both anger and desire showing in his eyes.

It would not be until the following day that Carver, thinking back more calmly upon the incident, would remember that Rebecca had been carrying both food and rolled bandages in her bag. And would idly wonder why.

A full moon blazed down over the great valley as the solitary rider crossed one of the sturdy stone bridges built by the Brethren over the Holy Water River, then continued on up along the climbing trail leading to the High Chapel.

As Rebecca approached the building the front door opened and Fallon stood on the steps watching her ride in. Their greetings were wary today. A man living in the shadow of the noose had to be suspicious of everybody, even someone who'd saved his life. And Rebecca, the innocent child-woman of an unworldly environment, could not help but feel a little nervous alone in the presence of a man said to have murdered his own wife.

She'd brought food, drink and medical supplies. But no tobacco. Tobacco was forbidden in the valley, as was strong drink.

'Don't know if I'm going to survive

without a smoke,' Fallon joked, poker-faced. Yet he half-meant it. The fugitive was a simple, hard-working man of the land hurled headlong into the violently different world of the fugitive. As such, he knew what was good for him and what wasn't. Tobacco had long been his his comfort and curative.

Then he grinned and shrugged. 'But I'll get by,' he insisted, seeing her disappointment. He took the basket. 'Much obliged, Becky, although you shouldn't be taking risks like this.'

She studied his face intently, shrewdly. Something was different, she realized. Something suggested by a twinkle in his eye, the hint of a smile at the corners of his mouth. She frowned. What on earth could he find to smile about — a man hunted and hounded like a wild animal with an injured limb to add to his woes?

She started when he suddenly held out his walking stick as though expecting her to take it. She made no effort to do so, frowning at him uncomprehendingly.

He grinned broadly and tossed the stick away. Then casually and with barely a hint of a limp, walked after it and retrieved it before turning back with an expectant grin on his face.

'*Voilà!*' he said. 'Ain't that what the magicians say in the travelling shows?'

'My goodness!' she cried, clapping her hands. 'You aren't limping, Jack. But . . . how?'

He explained what had occurred, and she squeezed his hand. He returned the pressure and she blushed and quickly drew away.

'Tell me about it while you eat, Jack. You must be starving.'

He surely was. Even so he ate sparingly after they'd repaired inside. As soon as he'd finished he patted his pockets in an habitual gesture which Rebecca identified as that of a smoker feeling for the makings.

She smiled understandingly and passed him an apple. 'Father was a heavy smoker before he gave it up as he did just about everything else when he joined the Brethren. But perhaps I could get you some, if you'd like me to?'

He frowned.

'How could you do that?'

'Francine and I are to be allowed to visit Woodstock with the menfolk shortly. The women go in on rotation every few weeks.'

'Why, that sure would be fine.'

She frowned. 'There might be an obstacle though, Mr Fallon. You see, we womenfolk aren't actually permitted to possess any money . . . '

He nodded understandingly. Another restriction! These holy-rollers lived in some kind of Dark Ages. He'd like to set all these girls, women and old ladies free, but knew this was just empty day-dreaming. He couldn't help anybody — would be damned lucky to get out of here alive himself, never mind anything more challenging than that.

'No trouble,' he smiled, digging into his Levis to produce a handful of gold coins, double eagles. They had been so eager to hang him down in San Pedro they hadn't even taken time to search him or his belongings. 'Take this. You might get me a flask of rye as well, so long as it's not dangerous?'

She slipped the money into the pocket of her sombre dress then lifted his right foot onto her lap and began expertly removing the strapping.

'I shall do my best,' she promised. 'My! Look how that swelling has gone down.'

Fallon studied her bowed head as she worked liniment into his ankle. Then he heard himself quietly say, 'I didn't do it, you know?'

Rebecca looked up sharply. 'I . . . beg your pardon?'

He smiled wearily. He was strong and resourceful by nature, yet the events of the past two weeks had drained him as never before. The death of his wife, the arrest and trial followed by the aborted hanging, culminating in his escape and flight, seemed like a blurred nightmare. An ordinary life transformed into chaos

. . . yet still a life he meant to salvage and make mean something again.

'I can tell you've heard all about me,' he said quietly. 'I guessed it the moment you rode into sight.' He spread his hands. 'All I can tell you is that I didn't do it.'

'Do you want to talk about it?'

'No.'

He watched her finish her chore and begin packing her things. 'You'd better not come here again. It's too dangerous. The law can hang you for giving aid and comfort to a fugitive, you know. I'm walking well now, as you can see. As soon as I see the chance I'll just drift out of the valley and take my chances on the outside.'

He paused, grinning wryly as he hefted his .45. 'I was never much good with one of these but I reckon now's the time to get in a little practice . . . '

'I shall be back tomorrow night, Mr Fallon,' she said firmly, rising.

'Why should you?'

'We're taught here to love our fellow

man, the sinners along with the saints. And I don't believe any man should ever hang, no matter what he has or hasn't done.'

'That's real comforting to know, girl. But I still reckon I got to go.'

'Tomorrow night!' Rebecca said firmly, moving down the nave. 'Please be here, Mr Fallon, for I fear that if you were anywhere else you might well be dead.' She paused in the archway to pose a surprising question. 'Did you love your wife?'

'Yes.'

Fallon did not hear her start up and lope off down the trail a short time later. Nor did he notice the fat moon hanging in the sky or smell the watery scents coming up to him on the night wind.

Did you love your wife?

The words brought back the pain. For he'd loved her since the moment he'd first set eyes upon her until the day he'd ridden home to find her lying dead with a broken neck. He still loved her and always would. And in his secret soul he was at times almost regretful that somebody unknown had aborted his execution and given him the chance to escape. For had these events not occurred he would be dead now and his pain would be all over.

'Penny,' he whispered. But there were only plaster saints and bright-eyed spiders to hear.

4

Don't Count The Cost

'Stop!' roared the marshal. 'Stop in the name of the law!'

The man kept running, plunging headlong down the steep slope and plainly toting a rifle. Instantly St George threw his rifle to the shoulder and fired. The bullet ripped up a geyser of earth almost under the running man's feet.

'The next won't miss!' he shouted. 'Freeze, varmint!'

But again he was ignored. The ragged runner was making for the timber above his cave in the hills and it was now less than a fifty yards uphill climb. But before St George could trigger again Sheriff Dolan deliberately cut his mount across in front of him to block his line of fire. 'I don't believe that's your man, Marshal.'

'Get the hell out of my firing line!' St George snarled, and opened up.

His first shot missed, but not the next. The running figure fell with a sharp cry, tried to rise, but couldn't make it. St George heeled his big horse upslope. The wounded man lifted his rifle and squeezed trigger. The bullet took the marshal's horse in the chest. The animal grunted, stumbled a short distance then crashed down flinging the marshal through the air, arms flailing. He fell hard.

The possemen scattered as more wild shots came scorching down the slope. But not St George. Up on one knee now and smothered in dust, he fired the repeater from waist level, raking the ridge crest with lead. Recklessly, the distant figure sprang up again to make for the trees. St George pressed the rifle's oaken stock to his cheek, drew a fine bead and squeezed the trigger.

The man threw up his arms and fell backwards, almost disappearing in the long grass.

'Got him!' St George panted, and was up and running while his men were still warily clinging to cover.

The dead man was not Jack Fallon.

Sprawled in the grass, he was much older than the fugitive although build and colouring were similar.

St George was hunkered down on a boulder nearby when Dolan and the others rode up.

'I warned him fair,' he said defensively. 'I called on him in the name of the law but he kept running. Why did he do that?'

The sheriff had the answer. 'This here is Dooley James, Marshal,' he supplied, swinging down. 'Guess he must've figured we was after *him*.'

'Why in hell would he think that?' St George was testy. One of his possemen had been killed in a fall from his horse on the first day of the manhunt. Now he'd shot some nobody dead. None of this was going to look good in his report to head office in the county capital.

'It was on account Dooley was a fugitive himself,' Biff Dolan replied. 'Stole Jack Snapes's bay mare a coupla months back and has been hiding out ever since.' He stared accusingly at St George. 'There was a reward of just one hundred dollars on Dooley's head. That's how poor a small-timer he was.'

St George merely shrugged, hard-faced. His attitude was that one lousy horse thief here or there wasn't any great loss to his way of thinking.

'We're just wasting time,' he stated, rising and dusting off his rig with his hat. 'Give me a stirrup, Deputy. Your horse can carry double until we reach the next spread. I'll borrow a mount there and we'll push on to check out those holy rollers you had trouble with yesterday. What are they called again?'

'The Brethren,' Deputy Slater supplied as St George filled leather. He indicated the dead man. 'What about Dooley?'

'What about him?'

'We cain't just leave him here,

Marshal. It wouldn't be fittin'.'

'Would he have done anything for me if he'd killed me and not my horse?'

'Well . . . '

'Like hell he would! Let's go get my gear, Deputy. We are wasting time.'

The sheriff of Woodstock appeared pensive as they followed the double-laden horse down the slope. 'You know,' he remarked to a posseman, 'I don't reckon I ever saw anybody as mortal set on catching a man as your fire-breathing marshal is. Has he always been this way?'

'Reckon not, Sheriff,' the weary posseman answered. 'No, I reckon you could say the marshal sees this Fallon as something special.'

'Mebbe he is at that?'

★   ★   ★

The mug of buttermilk was perched precariously upon the deacon's black-robed knee. The hour was late but his hosts didn't really mind. It was always an honour for Elder March and his wife to have the leader of the Brethren come visit them in their home.

The mother felt doubly honoured tonight because of Deacon Brown's obsession with their daughter. It would be a feather in their caps when she became Deacon Brown's wife number three in just a few days' time. For Carver Brown had long had eyes for Becky, and while respectful of the Brown family as a unit, Elder March would sooner see his daughter marry a rattlesnake than Carver.

Elder March was no admirer of Carver Brown and was not alone in this amongst the Brethren.

The deacon's eyes kept straying to the gloomy hallway which led off the front room. Along that hallway was Becky's room. The ageing suitor envisioned the girl sleeping: rosy, lovely, virginal. It was difficult to keep his attention on what he was saying, but because he considered it important, he somehow managed it.

'I feel I have been everywhere God has land,' he declared in the flowery way he had at times. 'And based upon that experience I believe that all the people I've ever met can be placed in one of two categories. Those who love the Lord and unquestioningly follow his teachings, and those who are dominated by love of self.'

'Amen,' murmured Elder March.

'You most excellent people plainly fit into the first category,' the deacon continued, and the couple smiled and nodded in happy pride. His expression turned righteous. 'But it grieves and saddens me, that as of today, I am forced to believe that my own son has seemingly fallen amongst the latter.'

They'd expected him to get around to this. Carver Brown's increasing defiance of his father had shocked some of the Brethren of late. Carver had always been headstrong, outspoken and aggressive, yet this was the first time he'd dared challenge the deacon so blatantly.

'Just look at him right now,' Brown invited bitterly, following a weighty pause. 'What you see on the outside is supposed be a manifestation of his devotion to me. But I know the truth of it. He is watching me constantly for signs of weakness and senility. He's searching for this weapon to use against me while playing the role of the devoted son. If you fine folk have never seen naked hypocrisy walking and breathing, then feast your eyes now!'

The couple dutifully looked. Sure enough, directly across the square Carver Brown was to be seen now pacing to and fro with hands clasped behind his broad back and his big, dark head angled downwards as though in prayer. But as all the valley knew, Carver was not a prayerful man.

Matronly Mother March was kind, however. 'But perhaps it is genuine concern for his father that keeps him abroad at such an hour, Deacon? After all, those possemen were back at the entrance gates again tonight, so I am told. Perhaps Carver fears they might attempt to force their way in and cause alarm and unrest amongst us?'

The deacon rose, features stern. It was true that three possemen including the marshal of San Pedro himself, had been stopped at the gates earlier that night. He'd ordered his own sons to turn them away. It was reported Marshal St George had been very angry. The deacon might have worried about this had he not had more burdening thoughts tonight.

His overriding preoccupations were Carver's rebelliousness and his own lust for Rebecca March.

The deacon subscribed to the school of thought that nothing could help a man stay young like a young bride. He needed to maintain his youth in order to be able to stand up to Carver.

How ironical that Carver desired her also.

All the talk about the girl soon had the visitor in a light sweat and after some clearing of the throat and glances along the corridor, he asked if perhaps, as a special favour, the parents might ask their daughter to join them . . . just for a few minutes, of course.

'Surely not right now, Deacon?' Mother March said. 'But the dear child is fast asleep. It's almost the middle of the night.'

He'd worked on this speech and wasn't through yet as he seized the woman's plump hands and clasped them to his chest.

'Please, it is surely a simple request, Sister,' he pleaded emotionally. 'I am a man in love and within a few short days she shall be my bride. I hope and pray she will be as delighted to see me as I will her, even if the hour is late. As a special favour to your loving pastor, Sister?'

How could any loyal and pious woman like Mother March resist such a plea?

Smiling and sniffing, the dutiful woman hurried along to her daughter's door. She knocked, and receiving no response, opened the door and entered.

Her shriek drew the two men from the parlour.

They stared uncomprehendingly.

Rebecca's bed was empty and had not been slept in.

The resulting uproar brought Carver at the run from across the street, and even though the Marches were anything but admirers of the Deacon's son they had to admit it was reassuring to have him around in a crisis.

After calming them all down, Carver organized a hasty search of the stables where he discovered Rebecca's saddle was missing. The drowsy stable boy said he'd heard a horse leaving earlier and believed it had been travelling up-valley, heading north.

Upon hearing this Carver Brown suddenly found himself recalling his brush with Rebecca earlier that day and her guilty look when those odd items of food had spilled from her canvas sack. Coupled with her disappearance tonight, this was something plainly demanding investigation.

Right now.

'I'll go find her and bring her back,' he announced confidently. 'Saddle my horse!' he ordered the stableboy.

Naturally, his father protested. After all, Rebecca was the woman he planned to wed, therefore he should be the one to go searching.

'This cold night air isn't good for your chest, Father,' Carver said with mock solicitude as he swung astride. And as he rode off, had to add, 'At *your* age . . . for Pete's sake!'

* * *

It had been a good day.

His leg was virtually sound again and he felt completely recovered from his close brush with death for the first time. Apart from the craving for a good smoke and a double slug of rye whiskey, he was feeling boosted in spirit and almost at peace with the world as he paced up and down the chapel strengthening his ankle, while bright moonlight poured through stained glass windows and owls hooted in the deep woods.

Almost . . .

For in reality, the sense of danger here had never really left him. He was still a fugitive from the law, still risking becoming gallows bait should St George catch him. And he still had that nagging belief that the marshal would never quit until he was taken, no matter how long it might take.

He went outside.

Halting by the ancient elm which guarded the church like a sentinel, Fallon felt his concerns slowly easing from his mind as he gazed out over the sleeping valley.

As a man of the earth he had quickly fallen in love with this chunk of paradise hidden away in the mountain fastness. The air was like wine, the rich dark earth looked and smelt almost good enough to eat. In Resurrection a man might almost believe he could sow nails and harvest crowbars successfully in this beautiful soil. The valley's sheer size and richness made it appear a veritable dreamland to a hard-scrabble sheepman.

Fallon hoped the Brethren fully appreciated what they had here. He knew they'd had to fight to hold on to it. According to Rebecca those beyond the valley whom the Brethren called Outsiders were violently opposed to their strange and clannish style of living, while the one aspect of their religion the Outsiders found most intolerable was undoubtedly polygamy.

In a frontier land where Christian morality was enshrined in the hard line dogma of such accepted religions as Baptists, Methodists and Catholics, this radical departure from perceived nor-mality was repugnant and alien.

Fallon knew what it was like to be ostracized.

As the first and only sheepman to have survived in the cattle country around San Pedro he had been odd-man-out for years. And because he'd dared be different he'd had legal battles, stand-up fights and even shots fired at him in the night in attempts to get rid of him.

He smiled toughly, sobered again.

Maybe choosing to raise sheep in cattle country and subscribing to polygamy were totally unconnected, he was forced to concede. And yet surely the principle was the same. He believed every man should be free to live however he pleased in God's own country and figured these Brethren felt exactly the same.

The first sound of hoofbeats was barely audible, like the beat of a distant drum. He turned and stared south to pick out Rebecca's buckskin eventually as it emerged into the open below.

As she started up the hill Fallon climbed a rock pile and waved. He saw her eyes widen with relief when he jumped down and headed down to meet her with barely a suggestion of a limp.

For the first time since losing his wife

Jack Fallon was genuinely smiling as she reached his side and swung down. In that moment he was vividly aware of how close he'd come to death and just how good it was to be alive.

'I was afraid you mightn't come up tonight,' he said.

'I had to sneak out. I brought some food.'

'No tobacco or whiskey?' he joked.

'I'll try and get you some tobacco in Woodstock. But I don't know about alcohol.' She hefted the sack. 'Hungry?'

'As a bear.'

'Then why don't we go inside and I can fix you something.'

'It's kind of nice out here, don't you reckon?'

'It's beautiful. But it's also a little exposed. There's no regular nighthawk here up high in the valley, yet you can never be sure who might ride by. Are you fit enough to tie up the pony?'

He was, and did. By the time he entered the chapel the meal was ready: a cold haunch of goat, cheese, a canteen of fresh milk and a full loaf of cornbread.

Fallon ate heartily and listened attentively as she told him about Deputy Slater and Elwood Treece and the resulting brawl.

He swallowed a mouthful and nodded soberly. The Brethren weren't giving up, he realized. He was gratified to hear that the bullying Treece had been given a whipping, but that didn't erase the danger.

'It must really be terrible to be on the run and in fear for your life, Jack?'

He nodded, gazing at the window. Moonlight slanted through in golden bars that appeared almost solid. 'I don't want to die,' he stated simply. 'I guess it'd be bad enough if a man was guilty. But when you're innocent . . . '

She reached out and touched his hand.

'I don't believe you murdered your wife, Jack. I want you to know that.'

He took her hand and squeezed it. It was good to have at least somebody believe in you. Such support had been thin on the ground at San Pedro.

'I like you and I'm in your debt, Becky. But that's why we both of us know I have to leave now I'm mobile again. I've already put you in too much danger.'

Making no attempt to withdraw her hand, she spoke sharply. 'Now we'll hear no more of that kind of talk, Mr Fallon.'

'Jack. I like that best.'

'I really don't want you to go . . . Jack.'

'But — '

'Because *I* need you as well.'

He frowned, not understanding. He saw her face sadden and something bright glisten in her eyes as she looked down.

'Becky, you've got troubles too. What is it?'

She shook her head, golden curls catching the light.

'I have no right to burden you with my petty problems.' Tears ran down her cheeks to be swiftly brushed away.

'That wouldn't be fair.'

'Tell me. We're friends, aren't we?'

He had to be more persuasive, but eventually she gave in and told him everything: of Deacon Brown's intentions, her own revulsion at the notion of marrying someone forty years her senior, her parents' approval of the union and Carter Brown's lust and jealousy. Once started, the words rushed out. Yet talking seemed to help, he noted, for she eventually ceased crying so that by the time she was through she even managed the ghost of a smile.

'I'll wager you're sorry now you asked to hear all my troubles, Jack Fallon?'

He didn't reply. He'd thought he'd detected a faint sound outside, yet when he glanced sharply at the doorway, saw nothing. He turned back to her and took her other hand.

'You can't marry a man you don't love, Becky.'

'But I must. It's the law.'

'Brethren laws, maybe. Not real ones. Don't let them do this to you if you don't want it.' He grinned again. 'I'm a sheep rancher. So I know all about being stubborn, y' know?'

The unmistakable sound of a revolver hammer cocking brought him twisting about violently to face the doors. A broad-shouldered man with a black spade beard stood there holding a Colt, and Fallon heard Becky's shocked intake of breath: 'Carver!'

'Fallon!' Carver Brown growled, coming towards them. 'Yeah, I heard. OK, get on your feet, Fallon. You're in big trouble.'

As he rose slowly, Fallon's right hand brushed gunbutt. He could have attempted a draw, yet didn't. For one thing he was no dab hand with a Colt. For another, he didn't want to kill anyone — not even a man whose glittering eyes seemed to hold the sure promise of death.

5

Brute Force

St George's fist slammed into Blaine's chest and drove the man back hard against the corral fence. As the marshal lunged in to follow up his advantage, Hudson thrust out a foot, causing him to trip. He was falling when Blaine fetched him a slamming punch to the side of the head, jolting his Stetson loose and half-stunning him.

'Goddamnit, let that be enough of this, Marshal St George,' implored the third posseman, fat Judd Venner. 'This is loco, us fighting like this amongst ourselves.'

St George rose to one kneee and sleeved his mouth. His eyes were wild.

'There's only one way to stop this fight and that's for you three sons of bitches to agree to stay with me until we find Fallon!' he rasped. 'Otherwise,

82

by God, you could stay here dead!'

Three lawmen stared. They wondered if St George was losing his grip. He'd always been a hard-driving man but nobody had ever seen him back up the way he was about Jack Fallon.

How come?

It was now over a week since Fallon had cheated the hangman down in San Pedro. Many of the original possemen had quit that manhunt in the past twenty-four hours, but St George was plainly determined to prevent any further desertions. Now he was resorting to force and threats to hang on to them, and Hudson, Blaine and Venner just happened to be the unlucky ones he'd been able to snare before they also flew the coop.

'We ain't fighting you no more but we ain't staying on,' Hudson stated emphatically. 'We're heading back home and if you've got a lick of sense you'll do the same thing, Marshal. All this business seems to have twisted your think box.'

'Hell, Fallon's just a dirty woman-killer,' weighed in Blaine. 'He ain't a traitor to his country, goddamnit.'

The marshal rose, jaw muscles knotting, eyes reduced to steel slits.

'Only a killer?' he snorted. 'What if it had been your wife he'd killed, Blaine? Or your daughter, Venner? Would you still want me to quit?'

Without waiting for response, he stabbed a finger at the three saddled horses standing by the corral.

'Unsaddle those mounts. That's an order!'

Venner made to move for the corral but tough Hudson halted him.

'We ain't unsaddling,' Hudson stated. 'We are heading home, just like we planned. Nothing you can say or do will stop us, Marshal.'

St George lunged forward and felled the man with a savage right hook. Mustering his courage, Venner flung himself at the marshal, seizing him about the waist. As St George attempted to beat him off, Blaine crunched a right hook to the side of his head. St George reeled sideways and Venner quickly dragged him down onto his knees. Hudson, also kneeling, lunged back into the affray only to take a brutal forearm jolt to the nose that broke bone and stretched him flat on his back.

The desperate marshal was fighting his way back into form.

A kick sent Venner sprawling. St George lunged erect and rushed Blaine, who lowered his bullet head and butted him in the chest. St George immediately imprisoned the man's head in a headlock, swung him about and rammed him viciously into a corner post, head-first.

That was the moment when Woodstock's sheriff showed up accompanied by his deputy and big Elwood Treece. With some difficulty the trio managed to prise St George's headlock loose of Blaine, leaving the man to collapse to the ground gasping for air.

Although groggy, St George continued to resist until the sheriff seized him and slammed him backwards into the fence with force. The marshal's legs gave way and he slumped to his knees with eyes still blazing, but plainly he was all through.

Biff Dolan was a strong man who would only tolerate so much — from anybody.

'Cut it right here and now, Marshal, or by glory I'm gonna report you to County HQ. You hear me?'

St George had achieved self control again by the time he'd struggled erect. For that threat struck home. He had always been deeply unpopular at County HQ where he was regarded as over-zealous, trigger-happy and less than honest by some.

He shook away restraining hands and adjusted his rig. His mouth was bleeding and he had a cut under one eye. But he'd suffered worse than this in his chequered career behind the badge, much worse in truth.

'I don't thank you for this, Dolan,' he said acerbically. 'You either, Treece. Was it you who went running for them?'

Elwood Treece, battered and bruised, shook his rough head.

'Didn't want to see you wind up in trouble you couldn't haul your way out of, Marshal,' he stated. He meant it. The man was one of St George's few loyal henchmen. The marshal's gang was how they referred to them back in San Pedro, and it was no compliment. St George might boast an impressive record but his methods were often questionable.

'No such thing!' St George shot back, still riled.

'Easy, Marshal, easy,' said Deputy Slater. 'No call for you to be sore . . . you mightn't even need any backing anyways.'

'Huh?' St George was puzzled. 'Why the hell not?'

'Just received this here from Two Dog Bluff,' said Sheriff Dolan, producing a blue telegraph slip. 'Better take a look, Marshal.'

St George snatched the paper from his fingers. It read:

HAVE IN CUSTODY
UNIDENTIFIED MAN WHO
ANSWERS DESCRIPTION OF
FUGITIVE FALLON STOP
PLEASE ADVISE STOP
SIMPSON SHERIFF
TWO DOG BLUFF

'So, what do you make of that, Marshal,' Treece asked eagerly. 'Sounds promising, huh?'

'Damn right it does,' St George agreed. He studied the possemen. 'So . . . go if you want. Who needs you? I can check out this *hombre* on my own. But if you think I'll forget what happened here, you're mistaken.'

'Does this mean you won't be paying another visit on the Brethren, Marshal?' Dolan wanted to know. 'I recollect you was pretty sore at them refusing to let us in and all.'

'Why should I fret about the Brethren if there's a chance they could be holding Fallon in Two Dog Bluff?' St George cut in. He gestured at Treece.

'Round up what men we have left and tell them to be ready to leave for the Bluff inside the half-hour,' he barked, and strode off for a final word with the local lawmen.

Dolan and Slater did not look pleased. 'Too bad, Sheriff,' Dolan muttered.

'Yeah. Mebbe I should have held back that message until we seen what he could do with the Brethren?'

Dolan and Slater were rednecks from the deep south who hated everybody who didn't conform to their narrow way of thinking. As such, they represented the majority of local opinion regarding the Brethren. The locals wanted the Brethren purged from their county and were looking to Biff Dolan to do it, but the man had found that task beyond him.

Dolan had had high hopes St George would prove the shock weapon in his campaign, and had done everything possible to encourage the manhunter's belief his quarry might be hiding in the valley. But now it seemed he'd lost and the Brethren had won . . . again.

On their way back to the jailhouse they walked past a poster nailed to a fence. It depicted a stern and sober Biff Dolan below the large caption which read;

VOTE DOLAN

The elections were coming up and such was the animosity for the much-married Brethren that it was possible Dolan and Slater might be voted out due to their failure to come to grips with the whole problem of Resurrection Valley.

'Looks to me we're gonna have to figure another way to get them Bible-bashers, Deputy.'

'Looks like it, Sheriff. And I reckon we better be quick about it.'

★　★　★

Whenever matters involving the Brethren's laws were raised publicly the entire population of the valley, with the sole exception of the sentries, was expected to attend.

The order was basically democratic and not even the deacon was empowered to act or adjudicate on an important case alone. The vote was all powerful in Resurrection Valley and eventually, after he had been fully examined then given the chance to speak on his own behalf, the vote would decide the fate of Jack Fallon.

'Another kangaroo court!' was Fallon's reaction when they explained it to him, and so he had not bothered attempting to tell them the truth about what had happened back in San Pedro.

For ever since the moment he'd first found himself staring down the muzzle of Carver Brown's six-shooter at the chapel, he'd been inwardly resigned to the fact that he would eventually be turned over to Marshal St George and the hangman.

He saw no good reason why a band of religious fanatics should follow any other course of action in dealing with a convicted killer!

He had to concede the Brethren made an impressive spectacle as they filed into their large airy church-cum-meeting hall in sombre black robes and yellow sashes.

Standing before the altar, which was totally concealed beneath heavy drapes for this meeting, Fallon studied the faces as the Brethren filed into their places. They appeared clean, well-scrubbed and pious. They certainly bore no resemblace to that rabid drunken mob who'd railroaded him in San Pedro.

This offered a faint ray of hope when he considered the fact that these people had not packed him off directly to the hangman in Woodstock, as they might well have done.

Rebecca and Francine were amongst the last to come in, seating themselves up front. Their arrival caused a buzz for it was already known that the two girls had broken the laws by secretly harboring an Outsider.

Deacon Brown was last to appear from a small room off the altar and wasted no time in declaring the hearing open.

Stern and impressive, he first identified Fallon to the whole gathering then affirmed that he was indeed the escaped murderer being sought by Marshal St George along with his possemen and the lawmen from Woodstock.

A murmur swept the assembly at mention of Sheriff Dolan and Deputy Slater of Woodstock. It was not a friendly sound, as the lawmen's reputations were far from good here.

The first witness called was Carver Brown who told the assembly how he'd trailed Rebecca March to the High Chapel where he'd succeeded in taking the prisoner into custody at gunpoint.

Carver's evidence was brief and factual. He offered no criticism of Rebecca, and Fallon remembered that this man wished to marry her — as did Carver's own father!

The girls were next.

Questioned by Elder Mortimer they revealed how they had rescued Fallon from the Holy Water River, and it was Rebecca who explained why they had chosen to keep his presence secret.

'We were afraid he would be banished from the valley as all other Outsiders have been. He seemed so alone and exhausted we simply took pity upon him.'

'And he also appeared gentle and kind,' supported Francine. 'Becky and I both felt Mr Fallon posed no threat to the Brethren.'

'Did you still share that view after you realized just who and what this 'gentle Outsider' really was, Sister?' Elder Mortimer asked weightily. 'After you realized that possemen were in the region hunting for a fugitive from the law?'

Rebecca replied.

'It seemed too late to tell the truth then, Elder.'

'It's never too late for God's sweet

truth, Sister,' Deacon Brown said censoriously. He was far from impressed, and showed it. The fact that his betrothed-to-be was involved in something which contravened the Brethren's laws was highly disasteful to this man of the Lord.

He scowled at Fallon.

'Very well, sir, it's your turn now. Would you care to get up on your hind legs and try to give us one good reason why you should not be turned over to the law of the land and hanged?'

A hushed silence descended as Fallon got to his feet. The gathering saw a strongly built man of medium height with an open, honest face standing before them. Upright and impressive, he appeared the very antithesis of a killer.

And yet, the very first thing he confessed was that he had been charged with the murder of his wife and found guilty.

'I didn't do it,' he assured. 'I can't prove it, but I did not kill my wife. On the day she died I was off hunting wild horses near another town with two friends from San Pedro. As we were riding home together we sighted riders quitting my spread, the Cross Hatch, yet thought nothing of it. I said goodbye to my friends then rode in alone to find my wife dead . . . '

He paused for a long moment.

'She'd been attacked and her neck was broken. When I reported the killing I was immediately arrested and charged with the murder by Marshal St George.'

'If you didn't kill your wife, have you any idea who did?' asked the deacon.

'I reckoned the horseman I saw in the distance appeared familiar. And later, when the marshal fought so hard to get me convicted I realized who it had been that day.' He paused. 'It was Marshal St George himself! He'd been to my house that day!'

A buzz ran around the big room. It was obvious the Brethren were having difficulty in accepting what they'd just heard. Yet Fallon had believed it then and did so now. There was no longer any doubt in his mind that the man he'd seen quitting his spread that awful day was Marshal St George.

'Are you suggesting that the reason Marshal St George has been hunting you with such dogged determination is because he knows you are innocent and wishes to silence you before you could incriminate him?' challenged the deacon.

'Yes.'

Fallon's tone carried the ring of certainty and he felt he'd made some headway. Maybe.

Then Carver Brown rose and requested permission to escort Fallon personally to Woodstock and turn him over to the authorities there.

Several speakers immediately supported this proposal. But Becky quickly came forward again to plead on Fallon's behalf. She asked why the Brethren should ever want to assist in any way the Outsiders who in the past had done nothing but harass and persecute them at every turn.

She insisted Jack Fallon be at least given a chance, then caused a stir by formally asking that he be allowed to stay on in the valley where he would be safe.

'He will surely die if we force him to leave,' she protested spiritedly, 'for the manhunters are combing the entire county. Mr Fallon is a man of the earth, strong and hard-working. I believe he could and would help us here in return for us saving his life . . .'

Fallon felt a renewed surge of hope.

'You would never regret it, ladies and gentlemen,' he assured emotionally. 'Or should I say — Brothers and Sisters?'

There followed a silence. Plainly the impact of what had just been said was having its effect.

Then, 'Do you claim to be a man of God?' challenged the deacon.

'Indeed I do,' he replied truthfully.

'Do you love your fellow man?'

'Of course.' Fallon paused, then quoted, ''If any man says, I love God, and hate his brother, he is a liar; for he that loveth not his brother, whom he has seen, how could he love God whom he hath not seen?''

The Brethren were agog. Plainly this was a man like themselves who knew the scriptures. The expression of pride and pleasure on Rebecca's face told Fallon his gambit just might prove successful. Might . . .

'First Epistle of John, Chapter Four,' Fallon added quietly.

'I've had enough of this,' Carver Brown snarled, rising and coming forward. 'I say this man is not only a killer but a fraud and a slick-talking hypocrite as well. I demand permission to take him back to Woodstock. I insist on it!'

'Carver, you are out of order!' the deacon thundered.

'The hell with order! I know what's right and what should be done.' His face flushed with anger, the big man came forward and seized Fallon by the arm. 'I'm taking him in!'

'You are not, Carver Brown!' cried Rebecca. 'You are jealous because it was I who cared for this man. And that is so unworthy of you!'

Everyone began shouting at once. Offended by the uproar the deacon hollered for order. Carver lost his temper completely and ordered his father be silent. He then made an attempt to drag Fallon out.

Fallon dug in his heels and swatted the big hand from his arm. 'Leave it be, Brown. This meeting will decide what's to be done, not you.'

'Damn you!' Carver snarled, and struck at him.

Fallon side-stepped the blow and retaliated. He was a work-hardened man who knew how to fight, and the Brethren witnessed an explosive set-to between the pair until Fallon landed a smashing right square on the bearded jaw. Carver Brown fell backwards and lay where he fell, out to the world.

Fallon was blowing hard as he stepped back. He felt certain he'd just lost any slim chance he might have had of winning the Brethren over. But he was reckoning without the deacon. Before the vote was taken, Deacon Brown addressed his flock for a solid quarter hour. He had warned the Brethren there could not be one shadow of doubt in their minds regarding Fallon's fate. He now boldly proclaimed the man should be permitted to remain in the valley for as long as he might desire; how to turn him over to the law of the jackals of the Outsiders would be tantamount to murder and a denial of their holy faith.

Not even the deacon's closest associates understood what lay behind this impassioned support for the stranger in their midst. Yet many noticed that each time the deacon glanced across at the battered and still dazed Carver, that sight appeared to stimulate him to even greater eloquence.

And they were right.

For the reality was that Jack Fallon was the first man ever to defeat the deacon's eldest son in combat. The truth was the old man had long been afraid of Carver and realized instantly that to have at least one strong man in the valley capable of standing up to his offspring might well prove a huge asset — for himself as well as others.

The subsequent vote went Fallon's way.

From that moment onwards, until he chose to leave the valley or a contrary vote was taken, he was an honorary member of the Brethren.

6

This is Not Fallon!

The prisoner was almost six feet tall, of husky physique with dark hair and blue eyes. He'd told the Two Dog Bluff lawmen his name was Willis, and this could be true for it certainly wasn't Fallon.

Spattered with the dust of hard travel and haggard from lack of sleep, Marshal St George lowered himself to a bench in the jailhouse and stared bleakly at the prisoner through the bars.

All this way for nothing!

'Sorry, Marshal,' muttered Sheriff Simpson. 'But I reckoned he sure answered the description of the feller you've been after.'

'He does. It's not your fault . . . '

St George leaned back against the wall and dragged off his hat. The legs of his trousers were coated with alkali and big patches of sweat showed beneath the armpits of his dark blue shirt.

'What now, Marshal?' asked Treece, the only member of the original San Pedro posse still with him. 'You gonna finally give up on Fallon now, huh?'

'Never!'

'Well, we don't have any more leads. What next?'

'We go back to Woodstock.' St George sleeved his brow. 'He's there someplace. He's got to be . . .'

'Well,' Treece said after a silence, 'I reckon I might as well stick with you. Somebody should . . . I guess.' The deputy didn't sound sure he was making a wise decision or not. He liked the excitement of the manhunt but not the brutally hard work involved in a drawn-out case like this.

St George just grunted and slumped in his chair, mustering up the strength to leave. After a time he realized the local lawman was studying him intensely. The marshal scowled and sat up straighter.

'Something on your mind, Sheriff?' he challenged.

'No . . . not exactly, Marshal St George. Just musing on the long arm of coincidence, I guess . . .'

St George's frown cut deeper. 'What the hell are you rambling about?'

Simpson was sorry he'd spoken, and the marshal had to browbeat him some before he would continue. He eventually produced some old files which he'd been perusing in the hope of finding out more about his prisoner. During the search he'd come across a description of a man wanted for the crime of rape, committed five years earlier in Texas. The detailed description of the wanted man, named Fargo, almost fitted Marshal St George to a T, and Simpson had been burning with curiosity ever since this discovery. St George scared the hell out of him, yet he'd just had to see his reaction.

Shaking just a little he handed the file over to his visitor, a single bead of cold sweat trickling down his neck.

For a moment as he confronted the page, St George's iron composure appeared to slip. In that sliver of time he looked uncharacteristically vulnerable and unsure. Yet next instant he was himself again, the self-assured man of the law who didn't suffer fools gladly.

'My father was the living image of Abe Lincoln, but he wasn't President,' he snapped, grabbing for his hat. 'I suggest that instead of wasting time on ancient files, Sheriff, you concentrate on bringing this dump up to standard or somebody at County HQ might well very soon receive a request for an investigation of your position up here. Get me?'

The sheriff was sorry he'd opened his mouth.

'Yes, sir . . . of course, Marshal. I'm sorry for . . . for everything and I . . . '

But the marshal had already left, Treece shooting the sheriff a look that said he considered him a fool. And even the man who was not Jack Fallon, managed a chuckle.

'Appears to me you ought to think about hobbling that tongue of yours afore it gets you into big trouble, lawman. That hard-nosed marshal didn't like what you showed him one little bit.'

The sheriff ignored him. He was poring over that Fargo description again, thinking about the marshal. This certainly was some coincidence.

* * *

It was a bitter surprise for Tyball Walsh to be told he was dying. Up to the time the San Pedro doctor made his diagnosis of liver disease the rancher had been feeling vigorous, aggressive and very much a man in charge of his own life and that of those around him.

'You're the greatest fool in creation!' he'd accused the doctor, thumping his brawny chest. 'I'll outlive you by twenty years, sawbones.'

But six weeks later Walsh was no longer beating his breast or bragging. Frail, sunken and aged almost beyond recognition, he lay motionless beneath the counterpane in his big old cheerless house, and faced reality. And this was, frankly, he had just about run his race. The medico had been right and the shadows were closing in.

His sons were in the sickroom — tall gaunt replicas of the father. The major difference between the generations was that Ed and Zeke Walsh were not mean, biased or venomously hate-driven as was the father. When Tyball hated he hated hard, and what he had detested most in his lifetime, was sheepmen. His life might be ebbing but his venom was as poisonous as ever.

He scowled at his offspring. Ed and Zeke, he had to confess with bitter regret, were decent, kindly and caring men. The old man couldn't understand where he'd gone wrong.

'So?' he rasped out. 'What in hell do you two want here?'

'Just stopped by to see how you're feeling, Pa,' said Zeke.

'Come to see if I'm dead yet, you

mean.' He knew his sons loved him but could never accept the fact. Cowboys on the spread described their employer as the meanest old son of bitch in all San Pedro County. The sons shared this view but never said so. They were too kind and decent.

'The work's going well, Pa,' Ed offered conversationally. 'We're running ahead of schedule at the moment, matter of fact.'

'So you tell me!' Another of Tyball's characteristics was that he never believed anybody, not even his sons, who never lied to him. He rolled his eyes, trying to focus on blurring faces. 'Did they catch him yet?'

'Who, Dad?' asked Zeke.

'That goddamn, murdering sheepman of course. Fallon. Who else?'

The brothers traded glances. Fugitive Jack Fallon was a sore point between father and sons. The two had been in Fallon's company the day his wife had been killed, yet had been prevented from giving testimony by their father.

Tyball had been stronger then and had threatened to disinherit both of them and kick them off the spread if they ventured within ten miles of the San Pedro courthouse that day.

'The marshal's still hunting Fallon up in the Roblais Mountains, Pa,' Ed supplied, 'although most of the posse-men have returned home by this time.'

'They're saying Fallon must be dead,' said Zeke.

'Good enough for him,' Tyball growled, then coughed hackingly.

'But others say he's given St George the slip,' Ed weighed in. He cleared his throat nervously. 'Which brings us to the reason we stopped by, Pa. Zeke and me figured that with you feeling so poorly and all, and the doc saying as how you could die . . . well, we kind of thought that mebbe you'd like to wipe the slate clean and allow us to go tell the law what we know before it's too — '

'Get out!' Tyball roared.

'But, Dad — '

'Out of this room and out of my goddamn sight!' bellowed the old man with some of the old vigour and venom. 'Git afore I call my goddamn attorney and write you both out of my will like I said I might. Go on, git!'

The brothers quit the room in haste and the shaking old man collapsed back on his pillows.

'Sheepmen!' he croaked. 'With any luck they'll snare that Fallon and swing him high afore I die. Damn me if that wouldn't almost make going tolerable . . . '

When it came to good, old-fashioned hatred, Tyball Walsh was right up there with the best.

★   ★   ★

Fallon sweated as he swung the heavy hoe.

It was mid-morning in the land of the Brethren and he would like to strip to the waist but that was not permitted here. At least he was far more

111

comfortable in shirt and pants than the other diggers in their robes. Yet none of them complained. He'd learned that complaining was another thing that was frowned upon in Resurrection Valley.

He was relieved to sight the women coming out to the fields carrying their covered baskets as this indicated it was time for the noon break.

Fallon rested his hoe against the fence along with the others and walked for the tree shade over by the storage barn.

There were eight of them chopping weeds out of the alfalfa. Two of the eight were probationers like himself. These were local men who'd been attracted by the Brethren either by the call of a vocation or the lures of a polygamous society.

Novices were tested out with hard labour in the valley. The belief was that this was the only way to separate the real converts from the bogus. The notion was that if a man could survive the killing work test and not crack, he most likely was genuine.

He believed the Brethren seemed to regard him as one of the genuine ones and he wasn't about to do or say anything that might change that view right now.

For the truth was he needed the security of this place right now. Sure, he was fully back in shape again, but at the moment had no taste for running again from the John Laws and maybe being called upon to use his gun again in order simply to remain free.

The former hard-working sheepman had been propelled into an alien world of danger and violence by circumstance, but felt here that he had earned a reprise.

Fallon paused to gaze over the valley. The sight of the noon sun shimmering over the alfalfa fields, rangeland, rolling hills and encircling cliffs made a man simply feel good.

It had proven a peaceful week contrasting strongly with those preceding. He'd worked hard and kept strictly to himself. The Brethren were all sworn to secrecy regarding his presence and he felt reasonably secure. His fitness increased by the day and his ankle had fully healed.

His one departure from Brethren rules was the Colt strapped out of sight around his right calf muscle and which he claimed to have misplaced.

He had vowed that before anybody would ever get to slip a noose around his neck — again he would fight to the death and take as many with him as possible.

And yet he prayed it would never come to that. The peace of the valley had seeped into his bones. There was a timeless feeling here that satisfied him deeply, even if there might be many aspects of the Brethren way of life that were strange and alien.

Yet a man could lose himself here, he mused as he walked, maybe forever.

'Brother Jack!'

The man who called was Matthew Brown, the deacon's youngest son. He was in charge of a work party and was beckoning Fallon across to the shade. As he responded he sighted the women coming around the north corner of the barn. Rebecca and Francine were among them.

Fallon found himself swabbing his sweaty face with his bandanna then slapping the dust from his rig with his hat. Although convinced he could never show interest in another woman after losing Penny, yet for some reason it still seemed important that he look at least neat and tidy whenever Rebecca happened by.

Matthew smiled a greeting.

'I was afraid you might stand out there so long you'd get sunstroke, Brother Jack. You seemed a hundred miles away.'

Fallon shrugged. 'Just day-dreaming.' He quite liked the young man yet couldn't forget the fact he was Carver's brother. There was no doubting Carver Brown regarded him as an enemy.

'You're making good progress, Brother,' Matthew said, dropping a hand on his shoulder. 'We're well pleased with your progress.'

'Obliged.'

'The longer you are here in the valley the more convinced we become that you could not be guilty of the foul deed of which you stand accused.'

'Does your brother share that view?'

Matthew dropped his hand with a sigh.

'Even Carver's own brothers are never quite sure what he's thinking or planning at any given time, Brother Jack,' he confessed. Then he flashed a smile. 'Ahh . . . see, the ministering angels are here. What a welcome sight for weary men . . . good food and pretty women. Come, my friends, we must praise the Lord and eat.'

Fallon was pleased when Rebecca seated herself by his side at the long trestle table set up beneath the oaks. He'd not seen her in a couple of days and had missed her company. But as they began eating he sensed the girl appeared troubled.

'Something wrong, Becky?' he asked quietly.

'Of course not. Why should there be?'

'Just asking.' He grinned. 'You shouldn't be snappy, Becky. Crankiness is a sin here, isn't it?'

'Everything is a sin in this place,' she muttered unsmilingly.

Fallon studied her profile for a long moment. 'I can tell you're not happy. Why don't you tell me about it?'

'What could you do about it? What could anybody do?'

His raised dark brows. 'The deacon?' he guessed.

She stared down at her plate. 'He came calling again last night. They were finalizing the wedding arrangements.'

Fallon wasn't smiling any longer. 'So?'

'So?' she echoed sharply, looking up. 'So — how would you feel about marrying someone forty years older than yourself, Jack Fallon?'

'Not so good, I guess. But you could always refuse.'

'If only I could.'

'You mean you can't?'

'It's expected of a woman that she should always do what the deacon, the elders and her parents wish. And they all wish for me to marry him.' She shrugged fatalistically. 'My life would become a misery were I to try to refuse. It would not be worth it.'

'But, damnit, that sounds almost like slavery!'

'Yes,' she said quietly. 'Doesn't it?'

The remainder of the mealtime passed in silence, Becky scarcely eating, Fallon deep in thought. But when it came time to break up the girl brightened a little. She revealed she was going into Woodstock next day and would do her best to procure his tobacco. She still had the money he had pressed upon her up at High Chapel.

He grinned. 'You know, maybe I've forgotten how to smoke by now?'

She smiled wistfully. 'It must be so pleasant to have a vice. Luxurious.'

He laughed. 'Believe me, I have more

118

than just one . . . '

His voice trailed away. Carver Brown had just ridden up, broad-shouldered and stalwart astride a barrel-chested black horse around eighteen hands high.

The man didn't speak at first and Fallon found himself studying him thoughtfully.

Carver Brown was a man who rarely smiled and seemed to draw no pleasure from small talk or casual social interchange. Fallon had learned that the majority of valley folk seemed to regard him as the next deacon despite his arrogance and overbearing ways.

It seemed to him that Carver's strength and sense of purpose could carry him to the leadership when the time came and the ageing deacon stepped down. Due to the Brethren's slowly worsening relationships with the Outsiders it was generally agreed that the next deacon should necessarily be made of tougher material than Deacon Brown.

Matthew spoke to the silent horseman but he did not respond. His brooding gaze followed Fallon and Rebecca as they rose and parted, one to return to the fields and the other to go back to the village with the other women.

Fallon had been back at work for some time before he heard someone approaching. Somehow he was not surprised when he turned and confronted Carver Brown.

'Don't stop,' Carver ordered. 'There's still plenty to be done.'

'It's time I had a breather,' Fallon replied, deliberately leaning on his hoe handle. He didn't need a rest. It just seemed instinctive for him to oppose anything this man said or did.

Carver spread heavy legs and folded his arms. 'I'm going down to Woodstock tomorrow, Fallon.'

'Yeah?'

'Supplies.'

'Uh-huh.'

'I'm told that the marshal is still about some place.'

'So?'

'There could be hell to pay if somebody told him we've got you out here, wouldn't there?'

'Are you saying you might?'

'All I'm saying is that somebody could make a slip like that.' He paused. 'But likely that could only happen if that somebody felt you weren't keeping in his place out here like you should?'

'Are you saying you might?'

'Well, you can never be certain what somebody's conscience might force him to do . . .'

Fallon's jaws set hard, his eyes glittered. 'No prize for guessing who that somebody might be. So, why are you telling me this, Brown? Why don't you just go ahead and blab about me? Seems to me you're craving to do it.'

Carver's face shadowed.

'I'm offering you a chance here, sheepman. Keep away from Rebecca and nobody will go blabbing to any Outsider marshal! But ignore my warning and you never know what could happen.'

Fallon folded his arms.

'You too, huh? Your own father is running after Becky, and so are you. Well, maybe she should be flattered by all the attention, but I've a strong hunch that ain't the case.'

Brown took two menacing steps closer.

'Step real careful, Outsider. Maybe you took me by surprise once, but I'd never let that happen again. The next time we clash, if there is a next time, you won't come out of it so well. And now —'

He broke off as Fallon suddenly swung his hoe. The blade bit deep into the earth an inch from Carver's foot. The man jumped back with a curse the Brethren would never condone. For a long moment the two stood face-to-face, the hatred raw in their eyes, locked in a battle of wills.

In the end it was Carver who quit. He spun on his heel and strode off over the furrows leaving Fallon to his work and his thoughts.

7

Could A Marshal Swing?

The Woodstock General Store stretched a full half-block along Main Street. The largest commercial establishment in town boasted a long front gallery decorated with brightly painted new pieces of farming equipment chained and bolted securely to the plank floor. Inside, counters and shelves were piled high with sacks and barrels and were festooned with hanging harness and saddlery. Other displays were piled high with knives, dishes, pots, pans, tools, traps, rifles and trinkets. A side area boasted a drug and liquor display and the air was heavy with the aromas of tobacco, whiskey and fat onions.

The store was a meeting place for loafers and Elwood Treece was one of the regular visitors that morning when the Brethren women entered the shop.

Although most of the San Pedro possemen had long since returned home empty-handed and played out, Treece was still hanging about with several other hardcases. A vicious idler with a mean reputation, the hardcase had not given up on the hunt for Jack Fallon and still hoped maybe to flush him out and grab a little blood and guts action before returning to the dull monotony of town life back in San Pedro.

A hint of tension pervaded the store as the pretty, dark-blue-robed young women moved about examining various goods on display. Although the Brethren were anathema to most towners the fresh-faced good looks of Rebecca and Francine ensured that they were far better received here than their menfolk.

Slouched on a stool over by the liquor counter, Treece watched the women with a blend of interest and lust. He was suddenly feeling better and enjoyed the lift in tension the visitors introduced into the store. Tension could often lead to violence and Treece was always ready for that.

As the women conducted their business at the tobacco counter, Treece glanced out the window. Several black-robed Brethren menfolk wearing their flat-brimmed hats were in sight upon the gallery inspecting the new ploughs on display.

There was no sign of either marshal or sheriff. Rogan St George and Biff Dolan had quit town earlier to go check on yet another rumoured sighting of Jack Fallon.

Treece knew the marshal would be sore when he discovered he'd missed an opportunity to confront some Brethren here in town. But St George was on the move as usual, still unconvinced Fallon wasn't holed up someplace up in Resurrection Valley.

The two women were moving slowly towards the doors after paying for their purchases. Treece saw the clerk curiously examining the coins they'd paid with.

'What've you got there?' he demanded, sliding off the stool and crossing to the tobacco counter.

The clerk shrugged. 'Paid me in double eagles, so they did. Mighty unusual.'

Treece felt his scalp tighten as he studied the coins. It was known that on his return to his ranch outside San Pedro, the day his wife died, Jack Fallon had been in possession of a considerable sum of money in double eagles as the result of a sheep sale at Sin River.

The hardcase hurried after Rebecca and Francine and caught up with them in the doorway.

'Just a minute there, you gals,' he said roughly. 'Where'd you get them there coins I just seen?'

They tried to ignore him. But Treece was persistent and pushed ahead to block the exit.

'I wanna know,' he said aggressively. 'C'mon, tell me how you came by them coins afore I get sore.'

Treece's raised voice was attracting attention. Brethren began converging on the store as did idlers and loafers from the nearby Frontier Saloon. Mayor Wilkes had been on the sharp lookout for trouble ever since the Brethren's arrival. Flanked by Cosgrove from the bank and Hudson the liveryman, he mounted the store's long front gallery with a frown. With the sheriff out of town the mayor wanted to avoid any trouble with the Brethren who, although supposedly gentle men of the cloth, had in the past proved themselves anything but weaklings.

'Treece!' called Wilkes. 'What's going on?'

While Treece explained, the two girls again made to move off. Treece, convinced he'd lucked on to something significant, strode after them and seized Rebecca by the arm . . . just as Carver Brown was emerging from the shop next door.

The Brethren's reaction was instant.

'You! Take your hands off that girl!'

Treece's face twisted. Carver Brown was the man who'd thrashed him so convincingly out in the valley.

'Keep him away from me, boys,' he yelled to the towners. 'I mean to find out just what this gal knows about that killer.'

Men moved forward to block Carver's path but they reckoned without Carver Brown's fierce nature and brute strength. With a blur of lightning punches he felled two of the towners then stepped over them to reach Treece.

Treece reacted instictively as he grabbed Rebecca to use her as a shield. In a flash Carver reached over the girl's shoulder to secure a grip on the big man's ear. He jerked with all his strength and Treece released his grip on the girl, gasping in white-lipped agony. Carver's right knee whipped up and slammed into his groin. As Treece jack-knifed Carver smashed a forearm across the back of his neck driving him face down into the floor boards.

Two gaunt young toughs came charging along the gallery, eager for trouble. Carver evaded one and seized the other by the arm. He twisted viciously and there was a sickening crack of bone as the mayor's son crashed down in a writhing heap clutching a broken wrist.

The violence had exploded with such suddenness that for a moment nobody seemed to know what to do next — except Carver Brown.

'We're leaving!' he announced, herding his people ahead of him towards their horses and wagons nearby. 'And you towners forget about making trouble, on account what just happened here was self-defence, pure and simple.'

Wilkes exploded with rage. 'Why you stinking, Bible-bashing bastard!' he thundered, and clawed for the Colt on his hip.

Carver's six-shooter filled his fist so fast nobody actually saw him whip it out from the folds of his robe.

'You already have one scum son with a broken bone, Wilkes,' he hissed. 'I doubt you want a bullet in the guts to go with that . . . but I swear to God you'll get it if you don't drop that piece!'

The Colt .45 thudded to the floorboards for a blind man could see Carver Brown meant every word.

It was over that fast. Within minutes the Brethren party was on its way unchallenged, leaving resentment and humiliation rising in their dust.

Mayor Wilkes's face was white with fury as he knelt by his injured son's side. 'Well . . . they have finally done it!' he hissed. 'Those holy-rolling foreigners have gone too far!'

He booted Treece in the ribs to jolt the man out of his daze. Treece blinked through the blood smearing his face.

'Go find both the sheriff and that marshal!' Wilkes shouted. 'Fast!'

Although groggy and leaking crimson Elwood Treece hurried out, sensing that at last things were beginning to happen.

Forking a horse, he stormed away at the gallop, cheered on his way by every angry man in town. They believed the mayor had said it right. The Brethren had finally gone too far.

The high stone wall and sturdy timber gates between the cliffs protected the only entrance into Resurrection Valley. Once, heavy pines and oaks had grown right up to the entrance but the Brethren had cleared all this away to provide the gate guards with a wide field of vision in the event of attack — always a possibility considering the current hostility of the Outsiders.

That night as a bloated moon hung in the sky over the Roblais Mountains the regular guard had been doubled. There were now eight sentries instead of the customary four, and that eight comprised some of the valley's very best men.

Jack Fallon was one of them.

He'd been surprised when approached by the deacon earlier to be asked if he was willing to do sentry duty. In light of the incident at Woodstock and the possibility of repercussions the deacon wanted the best personnel available to stand the night watch, and was firm in the belief that this should include Fallon.

Of course, as the deacon had explained, his not being a bona fide Brethren meant he was not obliged to agree, yet they would certainly be grateful if he did.

Fallon had not hesitated. It was very much in his own interests that valley security be maintained.

Pacing the well-worn elevated pathway on the valley side of the gates now, Fallon encountered Elder Mortimer and Aaron Brown with rifles slung over their shoulders. As he approached the entrance he sighted Carver talking with Matthew. Naturally Carver was in command of the guard detail, but Fallon found no fault with that.

The brothers fell silent at his approach and he sensed they'd been discussing him. Carver motioned Matthew away then leaned back against a massive gatepost, arms folded, jaw set. Jack paused before him and fixed him with a questioning look, then made to move on.

'Fallon!'

He paused. 'What?'

'Don't do it again.'

'Do what?'

'Force the Brethren to break their laws for you.'

Carver knew about the tobacco, Fallon realized. 'Seems to me that breaking some fool law against tobacco wasn't half as stupid as busting a man's arm. Why in hell did you do that?'

'To remind them once again that we're no white-fingered bunch of Bible-bashers, of course.' The man jerked a thumb over his shoulder. 'They'll get far more serious proof of that if they show up here tonight.'

'You're hoping they will, aren't you?'

'Why should I?'

'Beats me. Maybe you are figuring that if a shooting war breaks out and you come out on top the Brethren might decide you should take over as deacon?'

'Who'd want that job?'

'You would. Do you know why?'

'Why don't you tell me?'

'Because then you'd outrank your father and he wouldn't have first call on Becky any longer.'

Carver Brown's dark face twisted. 'Keep digging, mister, keep digging!'

'Digging?'

'Your grave with your mouth. For that is surely what you are doing.'

'Spoken like a true man of God!'

'Don't give me that hogswill. A man of God is no different from any other man. If he's not prepared to fight for what he's got he deserves to go under.'

Fallon shrugged and made to move on. But the other's words caused him to pause. 'Keep out of sight if trouble breaks, Fallon. Don't show yourself unless things really get out of hand. They might figure you're out here with us but there isn't anything to be gained by them knowing that for sure. You could be our surprise weapon.'

He moved off without reply.

The moon blazed down as he continued on to where the man-made wall had been cemented to the cliff. There he rested a spell before climbing up to a ledge from where he could survey the terrain on either side of the gates. He rolled and lighted a smoke, careful to keep the tiny glow well-hidden with cupped hands. He was grateful to Rebecca for getting him the tobacco even if it had caused some trouble, for he nursed a strong hunch that nothing would stop St George from showing up here now, and tobacco was always a good ally in a fight. Smoke trickling from his lips he watched Carver Brown pace impatiently to and fro before the tall gates, a man eager for battle.

* * *

The murmur of drunken voices and flickering patterns of lamplight spilled out from the jailhouse windows as the marshal studied the double eagles in his hands.

'Well, there's no telling one of these

coins from another,' he stated finally. 'But the fact that the Brethren girl paid the storekeeper with a pair of double eagles is more than enough for me.' He glanced up sharply at Treece, Sheriff Dolan, Deputy Slater and Mayor Wilkes all standing close by. 'Uh-huh, I accept this evidence as proof that Fallon is likely someplace in Resurrection Valley, probably under the protection of the Brethren.'

Elwood Treece smiled broadly. He held a bottle in his fist and the strong scent of whiskey pervaded the room.

Outside, the town was in the grip of anti-Brethren fever, a mood fuelled by wild talk and any amount of booze. Something raw and unquenchable was rising from the dust of Woodstock, stirring its citizenry to anger and violence.

The Brethren were far too strange and different for the plain folks here.

That was at the heart of their resentment, he knew. The holy people were strange in appearance, habit and in what they believed, therefore they should be hated and deserved to be destroyed. Hick town thinking.

Yet even if Woodstock was inflamed by the day's events the towners still needed the support of the formidable marshal from San Pedro. Nobody reckoned the Brethren would prove to be a pushover yet were ready to believe that just having Marshal St George leading them into action would swing the odds heavily their way.

'Does this mean we ride out to that damned valley now, Marshal?' Treece pressed.

St George rose from the desk and moved to the open doorway where his sudden appearance drew cheers from the crowd. Although this was Sheriff Dolan's town, nobody, Dolan himself included, had any doubt who was really in charge right now. The San Pedro lawman had been viewed in that light ever since his arrival.

'That depends,' St George said at length, 'on just how much grit your people have in their gizzards, Sheriff Dolan.'

Dolan moved forward to stand at the marshal's side. Before them, red-faced towners brandished bottles overhead along with guns and torches. They started in chanting the anti-Brethren slogans they'd composed while waiting for the lawmen to return.

Mayor Wilkes, father of the injured youth and an unrelenting opponent of the Brethren, had supplied the free booze all afternoon supported by a steady stream of bellicose rhetoric. As a result the mob was now primed up and ready to go. All that was needed was leadership, strong and uncompromising.

'They will stick to a man!'

Dolan's prediction carried more assurance and conviction than he really felt.

'You can count on that,' he went on. 'These men have had their bellyfull of sin-ridden hypocrites who call themselves Christians. Sick of their arrogance and evil ways. They want them driven out of that damned valley once and for all, and know, as I do, that now is the time.'

He rammed a fist above his head and shook it, beefy face reddening.

'By God I've not known a moment's peace since this holy blight descended upon us. So are we gonna go help the marshal hunt down this dirty killer and deal with anybody who tries to stop him doing his duty, or ain't we? Let me goddamn hear it!'

The roar of agreement that followed shook the street. This mob was primed and ready to go. Dolan, mean and vindictive by nature, was glowing with satisfaction as he swung upon St George.

'Well . . . does that satisfy you, Marshal?'

By way of response St George strode across to the hitchrail and mounted up. When the mob saw Dolan, Slater and Treece follow suit without hesitation, they let out another concerted roar and quickly got mounted.

As he rode soberly down the street at the head of his noisy posse, St George drew both Colts and checked them out. He didn't expect anything to come easy out in the valley but was determined to be successful. Yet deep down the only outcome the marshal was really interested in was the capture of Fallon — he really didn't give a damn about the Brethren. Or the towners either for that matter.

He simply wanted Fallon and wanted him dead.

For the reality was that this man had not known a moment's peace of mind ever since the day Fallon had stormed out of San Pedro with hands still thonged behind his back and a hangrope trailing from his throat and fluttering behind him.

For only St George himself was aware that, given the opportunity and favourable circumstances, Jack Fallon had it in his power to see the marshal tried, found guilty and hanged for murder. Legally.

8

The Gathering Storm

Fallon jacked a bullet into the chamber of his Winchester as the sudden sound of hoofbeats carried to him on the night air. Moments later he lowered the weapon upon realizing what he'd mistaken for hoofbeats had merely been a clatter of ancient stones falling loose from the cliffs under a gust of wind.

His eyes narrowed as a dark mass of horsemen swung into sight from the direction of the Brethren village. As the cavalcade drew nearer he realized it was being led by Deacon Brown himself.

The defenders' sentries were clustered about the gates minutes later as the riders approached, Carver scowling darkly as he strode forward to confront his father.

'What's the meaning of this?' he

challenged. 'What are you all doing out here when your duty is to protect the town?'

The deacon stepped down and confronted his eldest son.

'It occurred to some of us, Carver,' he said with an edge to his voice, 'that should violence erupt out here tonight you just might be tempted to take the easy way out and turn Brother Jack over to our enemies. I realized I had to come to warn you against any such course of action.'

A thick silence came down as Carver Brown slammed a fist into his palm. Only the eldest son and his father were aware that a major power struggle had blown up between them recently, dating back to about the time Jack Fallon first showed. It was a battle Carver meant to win, and soon. A victory against the Outsiders tonight would give his ambitions to seize control of the Brethren a huge boost. But he wanted it to be seen as his triumph alone, the better to enhance his standing with his fellow Brethren should the leadership be eventually thrown open.

Secretly, Carver Brown had deliberately fanned the flames of the fires between the valley and the Outsiders in the hope of rising to the leadership — through battle. He certainly didn't want the old man seizing any of the credit he hoped to attract to himself if the shooting began.

'I'll conduct things as I see fit, Father!' he snapped with defiance in his tone. 'And now you and the older men should be getting back to the village just in case serious trouble should break here.'

The deacon flushed. This was both insolent and patronizing.

'Don't dare offer me instruction, Carver. I am deacon, not you. It seems you are forgetting that fact more and more frequently lately.'

'Maybe this isn't the time to argue this matter, Father,' put in Matthew Brown. He paused to glance about uneasily. 'I mean, if our enemies should

143

come then we should be on full alert, not squabbling.'

All nodded but Carver and the deacon. Both realized this was the test of strength they'd known must come . . . eventually. Each knew the risk of wrangling at such a time yet neither was about to give ground.

'There are far more important matters than the Outsiders,' the deacon said finally in a strong voice that carried to every listening ear. 'And I declare that this matter of your continuing rebelliousness is best resolved right here and now, Carver. I am leader and as such I'm forbidding you to turn Brother Jack over to our enemies, if that was your intention, no matter what the provocation or inducement. Is that clearly understood?'

It only happened rarely, but in that moment, Carver Brown lost control.

'By God and by glory, old man, you show more concern for an Outsider who is a convicted woman-killer than you do for your own kin and kind. It's my belief you're growing senile and are no longer capable of leading us, and so you force my hand. In the interests of the survival of the Brethren I hereby serve notice that tomorrow I'll formally challenge for the position as spiritual and temporal leader of the Brethren!'

'You are not strong enough or respected enough to do that!' the deacon blazed.

Carver thumped his barrel chest. 'I'm the strongest man in Resurrection Valley . . . in this entire county!'

Fallon moved. He'd climbed down from the ledge and had been standing back during the exchange but now came forward without haste to reach the deacon's side. He then turned deliberately and faced Carver squarely with the butt of his Winchester resting upon the ground at his side.

Carver actually gave ground before Fallon's threatening body language. Every man present could see Jack was ready to stand by the leader and against the son.

'By God and by Judas — !' Carver

hissed, but the older man cut him off.

'Enough blasphemy, Carver,' he said in a strong voice. 'There shall be no more of that and your incessant rebelliousness shall end here tonight. From now on you will discharge your duties as instructed and there will be no further talk of challenges. In short, my son, you will once again begin behaving like a true Brethren and not like an Outsider bent on undermining my authority. Is that clear?'

Carver Brown opened his mouth to retort, but thought better of it. For everywhere his glance fell it met an unfriendly face. The Brethren had witnessed his brief challenge and seen it fail. They were being called upon to make a decision and every face warned Carver they had made it, and it had not gone his way.

It was that crushing realization that saw Carver Brown bow his head, something nobody had ever seen him do.

His voice was low yet his words carried. 'It is clear, Father. I-I'm sorry.'

He wasn't anything like sorry, and the old man knew it. But what was certain was that the deacon had carried the hour and that was all that was important right now.

'I accept,' he said generously. He turned to the silent Brethren. 'And now we have more important matters to attend to . . . '

As he turned to his horse he glanced back at Fallon and gave a small nod that spoke volumes. He then swung up and led the group away.

They were still in sight when a lookout perched atop one of the great gateposts suddenly straightened, stared north, then hollered:

'Riders a-comin'! And by God and by glory — it's the Outsiders!'

★ ★ ★

They appeared swiftly around a bend in the trail, some twenty to thirty horsemen heading towards the gates. Several clutched burning brands and all were armed.

Without a word Fallon retreated to the ledge in the cliff wall above and behind the gates with his Winchester to watch the trouble draw closer. By this time the sentries were fully alert, while the deacon's party had moved off up a rise a hundred yards up-valley to watch developments.

Fallon's jaws clamped hard with his sighting of the stalwart figure of Rogan St George travelling in the vanguard of the riders. He thought most of the party looked drunk, but not the marshal. That wasn't St George's style. As usual, the man appeared tall, lean and tough with moonlight splashing over him and torchlight casting his shadow long upon the land.

Fallon caressed his Winchester.

Had he been a killer he might have drawn a bead upon the badgeman and blown him out of his double-girthed Texas saddle. But he was no killer and never had been. And St George knew that.

The parley that consequently took

place between St George and Carver Brown was anything but friendly. St George demanded access to the valley to enable his possemen to conduct a search for Jack Fallon, strongly believed to be hiding in the valley.

Carver replied, 'Permission denied!'

Immediately the possemen started in shouting and cussing, with several making mock passes at the gates on horseback. They were loaded for bear, Fallon could see all too plainly. Full of hate and rotgut whiskey, if he was any judge; the stink of trouble surrounded them here as acrid as gunsmoke.

'You people realize you are in defiance of the law, don't you?' St George now had to shout to make himself heard. 'We are entitled to use lawful force if you won't listen to reason!'

'I'd forget about force — or bluff, if I was you!' Carver Brown sounded calm. The man wasn't short of courage.

Some fool touched off a shot.

It came from the Woodstock ranks,

but there was no identifying the shooter. The bullet smacked into the gate mere inches from where Aaron Brown was perched with his shotgun. Instantly Aaron triggered back and the blast struck one of the closer riders.

'That's torn it!' Fallon muttered, and threw himself full length along the top of the barricade wall and snugged his rifle butt into his shoulder.

Down below, St George bellowed an order and a swarm of riders immediately charged the gates. There was a hot flurry of gunfire and within mere moments the impetuous attack was driven back. Yet almost immediately, lasso ropes were swung high to loop around the gate tops and the attackers were attempting to drag them open when a rifle erupted viciously from off to the right.

Fallon wasn't aiming to kill but he certainly didn't miss.

Three rapid shots saw attacking horsemen slump in their saddles with howls of agony. Instantly the assault faltered. But a raging St George proved capable of rallying his men and they quickly returned to the attack, pouring in a hot and heavy fire and shooting through the gaps in the gates and above the stone wall.

The defenders fought with a remarkable show of courage and gun skill — for gentle men of the Lord.

From his high position, Fallon stepped up his fire. Upon shouted orders from Dolan, two horsemen broke away from the main bunch and came racing alongside the wall to seek him out. Fallon knocked one out of his saddle immediately with a slug in the shoulder then drilled a hole through the hat of the other to send him veering away and firing wildly, yet no longer a danger.

At that vital moment the deacon led his men back to the wall from which point they added the extra firepower to the defence that was to prove the turning point in the battle.

One by one, and then in numbers,

the possemen began to break away and St George and Dolan couldn't hold them. Toting their dead and wounded they galloped away crouching low in their saddles, cruelly spurring their mounts to even greater speed as hot lead pursued them.

The hour belonged to the Brethren.

★   ★   ★

It was a bright and sunny morning with a gentle breeze wafting down-valley from the north.

Fallon and Rebecca sat upon a bench in front of the March house beneath an olive tree laden with fruit. Glancing up-slope between the branches they could glimpse the activity taking place in and around the meeting hall where the wounded Brethren were being tended.

The valley beyond the town lay calm and still. Fallon had never seen it looking lovelier and he was missing it already, even though he hadn't yet left.

He realized he would only miss some of the people, for despite their piousness and good works he'd found the Brethren pretty much the same as folks any place else — prone to unkindness, greed, lust, jealousy, pride and simple self interest.

He grinned and mused; likely just like he was himself, if he was to be strictly honest.

But the one person he already knew he would miss most of all when he had left was surely the girl seated at his side. He sensed Becky might miss him in return for she was plainly fighting back tears as she attempted to persuade him to change his mind about leaving — one last time.

'It's foolish for you to feel you must leave simply because of what happened yesterday, Jack. Open conflict between the Brethren and the Outsiders has been threatening for ever so long now. If it hadn't been the search for you that finally triggered it off something else surely would have. You should not feel all the violence was your fault.'

He appreciated both her words and loyalty. Yet she really wasn't making any impression for nothing could alter rock-hard reality.

Blood had been spilled here because of him. He did not believe the Outsiders would have had the courage to attack the valley had not St George been here to lead them. And the sole reason St George was here was Jack Fallon. There could be no arguing with this reality nor with his belief that as long as he remained here his presence would pose a threat to the valley and his hosts.

That left but one option: he must go.

Rebecca's mother came out toting a tray of coffee and Johnny cakes which she had baked especially for him. The deacon had told the village that Fallon had turned the tide of battle in the Brethren's favor at the gates, and as a consequence he was the hero of the hour.

'Please eat up hearty now, Brother

Jack,' the good woman urged. 'You look a little peaked today.'

'Anyone who weighs under two hundred pounds looks peaky in Mother's eyes,' Becky smiled, passing Fallon his mug. 'Shall we drink a toast?'

'To what?' he said.

'Why . . . to your long and happy life here in Resurrection Valley, of course.'

He looked away as the mother vanished up the pathway.

The breeze was brushing the distant alfalfa fields with invisible fingers. Beyond loomed the ironstone cliffs, brooding and precipitous. And above the cliffs, towered the eternal mountains, shining in the sunlight.

He rolled a quirley and tried to explain one last time.

The law would never give up on him, he insisted. Most likely the marshal was already drumming up outside help to deal with what he and Dolan might now be able to label armed insurrection here in the valley. Yet even if that did not happen he still could not stay on.

For in the eyes of the Brethren he would always be an Outsider and never to be fully accepted.

'But what about me, Jack?'

'You, Becky? What do you mean?'

'I need you here.'

In that moment she seemed very young and childlike. He thought of those coveting her: a sixty-year-old with two wives and grown sons, and a rugged brute of a younger man seemingly without a single trace of kindness or gentleness in his make up.

He felt deeply for her. But what could he do?

She was weeping when he finally went off to announce his decision to the Brethren. The deacon and Carver responded exactly as he had anticipated — the former pleading with him to stay and the latter assuring him manfully that he was doing the decent thing in quitting.

He left at sunset that night without any goodbyes. He rode out through the compound gates feeling at once relieved, unselfish and also strangely empty as he looked back over the great valley where he'd almost died and then had been brought back to life — in more ways than one.

★ ★ ★

It was amazing how swiftly everything could change. A half-hour earlier he'd been riding high, then without warning he was plunging back into Hell.

He was once again in the Jimcrack Hills, hunting wild horses with his great pards Ed and Zeke Walsh thirty miles from home when his wife was raped and murdered. He sweated and groaned and lived again through the days of his arrest and trial . . . the noose, the mob, the miracle of the sawn gallows timber . . . headlong flight . . . escape from the posse but not from the pain . . .

He jolted back to the here and now to realize he was sweating and trembling.

Would the pain never end?

Little puffs of dust rose behind the marshal's boots as he walked down to the Frontier Saloon where the menfolk of Woodstock were gathered.

The metallic dawn light sheened the lawman's clean-shaven features as he came to a halt directly across from the saloon. The lamps still burned. Dozens of weary horses all but filled every hitchrail in the town's central block. An imposing grey pig came grunting from an alleyway searching for scraps as St George turned his head to face the east.

The light was rapidly strengthening.

The night which had marked the possemen's defeat and retreat was over and a new day was on the march. Just how that day might evolve depended upon three major factors: the mood of the town; his own personal strength and resolve; and Jack Fallon.

St George felt secure enough about the first two. The mood of Woodstock — due largely to his own rabble-rousing rhetoric overnight, supported by Mayor Wilkes's generous supply of free liquor — was now even meaner and uglier than it had been the day the marshal had first led them out to the valley.

His resolve remained strong despite the mauling they'd received at the hands of the Brethren.

And yet darkness encroached upon the thoughts and emotions of the feared peace officer of San Pedro as he brooded on the past ten hours.

He'd learned that overnight a wire had reached Sheriff Simpson of Two Dog Bluff requesting added information on himself, Marshal Rogan St George. This was an alarming development but hardly a surprising one, for the lawman who'd first stumbled across that wanted dodger in his files concerning the Texas rapist, Fargo, had the stubborn look of a man who'd keep on at something like a dog worrying a bone.

St George, Fargo, still reckoned he was safe from any real danger, providing he put Jack Fallon six feet under

— fast. Only then would the man no longer present any threat concerning what had taken place at the Cross Hatch Ranch the day Penny Fallon had died — with his hands about her throat. There was simply no way St George could give up on Fallon now. The man had to be caught and killed — which was where Jim Hogue came in.

Prior to Hogue's appearance in Woodstock the marshal had been anything but optimistic about his chances of recovering Fallon following his escape. The Brethren had demonstrated convincingly that they could not be overcome head-on at the wall and there seemed no other way of attacking them, apart from summoning outside help, which St George simply dared not risk.

But Jim Hogue, a wizened and unwashed hunter from the Black Range region of the Roblais Mountains, had appeared like a beam of light in the dark watches of the night with his boast about a secret route he knew of into

Resurrection Valley.

St George came perilously close to losing his temper when Hogue flatly refused to reveal the alleged route he'd once discovered during a drunken hunting expedition, until his grimy palm was crossed with a large amount of silver — $500 worth, to be exact.

St George had been tempted initially to draw his .45 and give the grimy little extortionist six of the best at close range. But Sheriff Dolan had convinced him that Hogue, although venal and greedy, was generally believed to be mostly honest. If he claimed he had vital information for sale, it was likely true.

The marshal's breast pocket now bulged with banknotes. After much haggling, Joe Cosgrove of the Woodstock Banking Company had eventually agreed to advance him the required sum, on loan.

It was also said that Hogue was temperamental and was as likely as not to change his mind on any deal or agreement on a whim. And yet he found the man in an uncharacteristically genial mood due to all the unaccustomed attention and flattery coming his way. The rednecks of Woodstock were now as eager to mount another assault upon the Brethren as was St George himself, and suddenly it seemed possible this smelly runt might really hold the key to the success of such an enterprise.

The saloon was hushed as big money changed hands.

Encircled by whiskey-blotched faces, glinting weapons and blood-stained bandaging, runty Jim Hogue felt seven feet tall. He'd arrived at this nothing town as a smelly bum yet first light found him a wealthy hero of the common man.

'So,' growled the marshal, towering over him. 'Where is this pass?'

'I'll have to show you personal.'

St George's face showed a glint of triumph when at last he swung to face the mob.

'Hear that?' he shouted. 'I just paid this man $500 for what he knows and he's agreed to take us into that holy-roller valley that's been sticking in your craw and making you look like losers all over the county all these years. What do you say to that?'

The response was rewarding. There was cheering and jeering and glasses raised on high.

But the marshal wanted more than this. The attack he proposed for the valley was a gamble he could not afford to lose. For should the fugitive Fallon get to bust loose and maybe find his way to a big town with a straight sheriff who would listen to him, St George could easily find himself swinging off a gallows . . .

He injected genuine passion into what he had to say.

'What I want to know right now is how many men in this room are prepared to lie down and accept what a wanted killer and his psalm-singing henchmen did to us last night? And how many of you are there with courage and sense of duty enough to grab this second chance you've just been given? In other words, my proven friends and courageous fighters, I'm inviting every real man of Woodstock to ride with me — and step forward while the cowards and yellow-bellies stay where they stand to be seen and counted!'

The marshal was good. He knew how to deliver a speech that offered but two options — black or white. Ride with me or be branded yellow!

The technique worked even better than he'd dared hope now as his exhortation resulted in all but a shame-faced handful stepping forward.

'We won't condemn them!' St George sneered, indicating the minority. 'We'll leave that to a higher court.'

He brandished his Colt .45.

'And today we'll only be judged by our deeds in battle. If we fail again, then let there be silence. But if we triumph, and we will, let's be seen as heroes — the ones who finally purged our country of god-botherers and Bible-bashing scum who hate our guts!'

It was overblown but effective. He strode to the doorway and shouted, 'Death to the Brethren!'

The chant was taken up as the mob flooded out into the street to mount up.

'So far so good,' St George muttered to himself as he filled leather. He kicked his horse across the street to confront Jim Hogue. 'All right, mister, we're ready to ride. Just remember, if this pass of yours doesn't exist, you die. Do you believe that?'

Hogue only had to meet that formidable stare to believe every word.

'It's up there,' he breathed. 'I swear to God.'

'Then let's get to it!' St George shouted and, bringing his gun arm swinging forward, led them off at the gallop.

The roaring, rhythmic chant bounced back from the falsefronts of Woodstock as his hate-driven posse followed him out: 'Death to the Brethren!'

★ ★ ★

Fallon rode slowly through the forest towards Woodstock. He smoked as he travelled and the taste of tobacco only served to remind him of things he was trying to forget — Rebecca and all those good times he'd enjoyed in that strange but lovely valley.

He wondered if his Penny would understand how and why he'd allowed another woman to enter his life. He sensed she might, for she'd always been smart and understanding. She would know what it was like to be lonely, hunted and hounded and then meet someone who helped ease the pain of her loss just a little. But, of course, the friendship with Becky March wasn't serious . . . or was it . . . ? He knew he would miss her, wherever it was he was going . . .

He shook his head, forced his thinking to refocus. He still didn't know his eventual destination . . . only that his immediate one was Woodstock.

There was no point in his quitting Resurrection Valley unless the enemy knew it. That was, after all, the main point of his leaving. They had to know he had gone so that they would leave the Brethren alone. He hoped.

He glimpsed a drift of woodsmoke and the glint of sunlight coming off rooftops through the trees ahead. He straightened in the saddle. Time for care now, Fallon. The challenge was to make sure the towners knew Jack Fallon was quitting the valley without getting himself shot to doll rags in the process by either a bitter towner or a fanatical lawman.

His gaze cut west.

There was a vast and open country out there. A man could lose himself, change his name and appearance, start afresh and learn to forget. Sounded easy if you said it fast . . .

Woodstock seemed asleep.

That was his first impression as he cleared the last of the timber and reined in by the bridge to look over the town. There was barely a soul to be seen, and certainly no sign of the mob they'd turned away from the gates to the valley. A flag atop the hotel fluttered in the morning wind and the ring of a blacksmith's hammer on steel only served to emphasize the deep stillness.

What was going on here?

Although tempted to ride in and find out, Fallon was cautious. Instead he slowly circled the town until he finally glimpsed an old man, half-awake and crochety, making his way downhill towards the river toting a wooden water pail.

Fallon was met by a suspicious scowl as he rode up through the dew-wet grass.

'Who be you?' the old-timer challenged.

'Where is everybody?' Fallon countered.

'How in hell would I know . . . ?'

The oldster broke off abruptly on finding himself staring at the muzzle of a six-gun. Fallon didn't have time to bandy words. 'Where,' he repeated ominously, 'is everybody?'

The old man trembled. He looked fierce but was just an old bum who scared easy. He was one of St George's 'spineless vermin' who had passed up on the opportunity to join the mob that left town earlier.

He babbled out an account of all that had transpired before daybreak, almost clearing the place of its menfolk.

The blood had drained from Fallon's face. He'd got here too damned late!

'So — is there another way into the valley?' he had to know.

'Wal, Jim Hogue sure enough reckons there is. Say, who are you anyways, mister? You always this proddy?'

But Fallon was already gone. Cutting across an open field then crossing the beat-up bridge at the gallop, he began circling the town with his gaze fixed on the ground until he found what he was looking for: hoof-churned sign in the soft earth angling northwest — the direction of the valley he'd quit just hours earlier!

He followed the sign at the gallop,

riding with hands and heels as the sun climbed the sky to his right. In his imagination it seemed the horse's hoof-beats were hammering out the grim tattoo: 'Too late! Too late!'

9

Challenge The Brethren

It was intended to be a very simple ceremony involving only the bridal couple, their respective families, Elder Mortimer as the officiating minister and a handful of close friends.

It was indeed a small party, yet due to the modest size of the High Chapel it appeared larger once people were assembled.

The chapel held a special place in the heart of the groom, Deacon Brown, for it had been the first substantial building erected following the Brethren's coming to the valley. It was also where he'd married his second wife several years earlier, although he was unlikely to make any reference to that occasion to his third and far younger bride-to-be today.

Wives one and two were in attendance and didn't seem unhappy that their mutual husband was taking unto himself another bride. Polygamy was a Brethren tradition. Besides, the older women liked Rebecca March and thought her very pretty even though she was looking anything but her best on this her day of days.

Becky wore traditional white but would have preferred funereal black to match her mood.

The reason for bringing the nuptials forward was more political than romantic. The Brethren had just notched up an impressive victory under the deacon's leadership and he was riding high. He wished to maintain that momentum, particularly now Jack Fallon had gone, leaving him without his powerful support. The deacon believed that marrying Rebecca would enhance his status as a vigorous and capable leader and so head off Carver's ambitions to take over.

Desire, of course, played its part in all this. Yet both his survival as leader and the future of the Brethren were really the main drivers behind today's ceremony.

Soon everybody was in place and armed men paced slowly to and fro outside. Not present were the deacon's eldest sons, Carver and Aaron. Carver, in a fine rage, had flatly refused to attend and had insisted Aaron remain down-valley with him to oversee the defences in the event the towners should return. Only Matthew was present and he was kept busy trying to quieten and comfort Becky who was weeping even before the ceremony — and certainly not from joy.

'My dear Brethren, we are gathered here today . . .' Elder Mortimer began, and as he moved into his speech, Becky sniffed even louder. This drew a disapproving glance from Elder March for whom this was a day to celebrate.

'I was growing a little concerned about Rebecca and young Fallon, m'dear,' he'd confided to his wife on the journey up to the High Chapel.

'He's a fine upstanding fellow, mind, and I for one am quite convinced he didn't kill his wife. But he's still an Outsider whereas Becky will now be the bride of a deacon, no less. This certainly is a red-letter day for us.'

As always his wife agreed yet with private reservations. For she had grown fond of Jack Fallon by this time and had developed genuine respect for the man, as had the majority of the Brethren. She was sorry he'd gone but considering the fact that Becky had seemed much too interested in him she supposed perhaps this was just as well.

Becky scarce heard the words Elder Mortimer was intoning as she stared up at the statue of St Peter, vividly remembering Fallon slumped beneath it when they hadn't known whether he might live or die.

She thought it ironical that the High Chapel had been chosen as the wedding venue, for it was here that her memories of Jack Fallon were keenest.

She sniffed involuntarily and told

herself she must stop this and at least try to appear happy. A bride with red eyes was not to be countenanced even if she was desperately unhappy.

Elder Mortimer was warming to his work when three evenly-spaced shots sounded in the distance.

The ceremony came to a dead stop.

Three shots here was the signal for danger!

Matthew Brown led the rush outside where one of the sentries had clambered up onto the steep roof to command a sweeping view of the upper valley.

'Two riders coming fast!' he called down. He shaded his eyes with his hand. 'Looks like our scouts. They're sure burning horsehide!'

'What does it mean?' A woman asked querulously. 'What danger could possibly be threatening up this end of the valley, Deacon?'

Deacon Brown had no idea for none of them had any knowledge of that narrow secret pass that wound down the face of Black Range. Until an hour earlier that knowledge had belonged exclusively to one John Hogue. But after money had changed hands the secret way had also been disclosed to the hate-driven men of Woodstock, who'd just completed the ride down the secret track to reach the valley floor — every drunken rider armed for surprise attack.

The watchers from the chapel couldn't believe their eyes when they sighted the alien horsemen before their first scouts could reach them. The invaders came pounding around the base of the western cliffs in a stream, weapons glinting wickedly in the sunlight.

The sight caused every Brethren heart to sink. Outsiders in the valley proper for the very first time! And see! Already they were cutting the wedding party off from the high trail down to the village!

The hard-riding Brethren scouts confirmed their worst fears when they galloped up to the chapel and sprang down. They revealed this was the same mob that had attacked the gate the previous night. Nobody knew how the intruders had actually managed to enter the valley. But that was the least of their problems now. The reality was that the enemy was amongst them. What were they going to do?

It was up to the deacon to decide and he immediately declared the Brethren must stand and fight.

This created panic amongst some of the older women and grim acceptance in the ranks of the younger men as they crowded back inside the chapel to hold a hasty meeting. Only the prospective bride appeared calm and self-possessed. It would almost appear as if Rebecca March considered an armed enemy attack preferable to being joined in holy wedlock to an old man she didn't even like.

★   ★   ★

Carver Brown killed one Outsider with a bullet between the eyes and crippled another with a shot that fractured the man's thigh bone and knocked him from his saddle.

His marksmanship blunted the enemy attack and forced the Outsiders to veer wildly off the uphill trail. But the towners' numbers were superior and when they eventually formed a circle around the village their riflemen began laying down a brutal, consistent barrage that forced even real fighters like Carver and Aaron Brown to duck for cover.

A member of the Brethren, trapped in the barn by the swiftness of the onslaught, suddenly burst from a rear door and dashed wildly for the meeting house.

He didn't make it.

Big Elwood Treece and Deputy Slater, both primed on rye whiskey and hungry for action, spurred their horses in close and cut the man down, then continued to pump lead into his body even though it was plain he was dead.

'Death to the Brethren!' rose the chant, primitive and frightening above the blast of the guns. 'Death! Death! Death!'

With sweat coursing down his powerful face, Carver sprang to a side window of the town chapel, rifle at his shoulder. Ignoring a bullet that smashed the glass above his head, showering him with slivers, he drew a bead on Slater and gently caressed the trigger. The bullet smashed the deputy's spine. He tumbled to the ground and rolled before coming to a halt against a fence post. As he struggled to rise on lifeless legs Aaron Brown drilled two bullets through his chest and killed him.

This caused the chanting to cease yet served only to increase the fury of the battle as an evil haze of gunsmoke drifted across the village and the ironstone cliffs echoed defeningly to the mad roar of the guns.

* * *

It took a sentry's bullet slamming into the earth mere yards ahead of his galloping horse, to bring Fallon to a sliding halt before the gates.

'Goddamnit!' he roared. 'Don't you fools recognize . . . ?'

That was as far as he got. While riding in at the gallop he had been unable to hear the mutter of the guns. But the sounds reached him all too clearly now as he stared up at a pale-faced sentry. 'They're here already!'

'They?' the man called back. 'Who's up there, Fallon? We heard the shooting start a half-hour back but we're under orders not to leave our posts here, no matter what.'

Falstaff, Grenville, Lawson and Krebbs were all Brethren with whom Fallon had worked before. They immediately swung the heavy gate open for him and he rode on through. He appeared strained yet resolute as he sat his saddle with head cocked to one side to the sound of the guns. He dreaded to guess what might be happening to the Brethren and was sickened to think Becky could be in danger.

Yet he forced himself to appear in full control as he swung down just inside the gate. There was a drunken mob to deal with right here and he must remain calm and clear-headed.

So he rolled a cigarette as he quietly related to the Brethren all he knew. They gaped in astonishment.

'All right . . . so where's this other way into the valley then, Fallon?'

Fallon shook his head.

'I wasn't told. I even doubted it existed . . . but I reckon all that shooting proves it's there all right.'

'My mother and father are up there,' Falstaff groaned, panic in his voice. 'The hell with staying here. I'm going to help.'

'Stay put!' Fallon rapped.

Falstaff rounded upon him. 'You can't give me orders, Fallon. You ain't even a Brethren.'

'There's five of us here,' said Fallon, amazed how calm his voice sounded as he licked his cigarette into shape. 'It sounds to me like the village is under siege, meaning the rest of the Brethren might well be trapped. But we are still mobile and if we make the best use of our numbers then we can turn things around.'

Falstaff stared at him for a long moment. 'Y'know,' he said after a silence, 'maybe that makes sense . . . '

Grenville nodded. 'Sure it does. For one thing's certain, and that's that Brother Jack here knows how to handle things when the going gets tough.'

Fallon lighted his smoke and inhaled deeply. 'Forget about standing guard here,' he announced. 'All the trouble you men are expecting is down below in the valley. So get mounted and we'll head for the town.'

The Brethren traded stares. They were good men, for guarding the entrance was one of the most important responsibilities in all the valley. Despite the ominous sounds of gunplay elsewhere they were disciplined enough to want to remain here on duty. But Fallon quickly convinced them otherwise and the debate ended with Falstaff, Krebbs and Lawson trotting off to get their horses, leaving Grenville stroking his beard and frowning.

'I just recollected something, Brother Jack . . . something important. Seems to me we mightn't find all the Brethren at the town after all on account there was to be a wedding today up at High Chapel — the deacon himself and Rebecca March.'

Fallon went totally still. For a long moment he simply stared at Grenville until the man grew uneasy under his gaze and began to fidget. Finally Jack took a deep drag on his cigarette, sucked the smoke all the way down into his lungs then allowed it to escape slowly. But it didn't help. He still felt he'd been punched in the guts. Married! Then his brain began to unscramble of its own accord and he realized he had to accept what he now knew had to be reality. And why shouldn't he? He was nothing to her — just a hunted outlaw with a gun and no future . . .

Within moments he was again strong and clear in his mind. It was none of his affair if Rebecca married a dozen times. He had no real claim upon the girl. He must forget everything else and focus solely on her safety — on a day that seemed to be at risk of coming apart all around him.

'I'll ride forward scout,' he stated, striding for the horses. He was impressed by the calmness he heard in his own voice as he filled leather. 'We'll make it back to the town across the sycamore slopes and we'll keep low and quiet. But just remember if we run into trouble between here and there, it's them or us. Forget brotherly love and turning the other cheek today. One rule — get the Outsiders before they get you.'

The words had barely left his lips when a party of Outsiders galloped into sight further along the town trail. Dispatched by their leaders to check out the wall defences, the trio was startled to find themselves suddenly confronted by dark-robed Brethren and a powerfully built man they had never seen before.

Fallon instantly whipped out his Colt and called upon the men to ditch their arms. The command went unheeded. These Outsiders were fired up on fighting talk, whiskey and anti-Brethren bias and were eager for trouble. They went for their guns.

Fallon shot a man dead without turning a hair. He felt no regret. Becky was in danger. He was ready to do anything to reach her, to kill as many as he must.

The enemy scattered wildly as he triggered again but then Brother Sila Krebbs tumbled from his saddle clutching his arm. When the third hellion realized he was alone he dropped his pistol, whirled his mount about and fled back in the direction of the town at the gallop.

Fallon hesitated just a moment then raked with spur and raced after him. The towner was well-mounted, and hunter and hunted had covered a swift mile before Fallon drew within six-gun range, raised his Colt, allowed for distance and gently squeezed trigger.

As the gunsmoke cleared he saw the man had come out of his saddle and was rolling in the dust like a sack of grain.

The invader was weeping, badly hurt. Fallon sprang to ground, hauled him to his feet and swatted him twice with the gun barrel.

'I got a wife and three kids,' he bleated. 'What'll they do without me?'

Fallon's features twisted with contempt. How well he knew this breed! Heroes in a mob but otherwise yellow clear through.

'You should have thought of that before you came out here to try and murder innocent women and kids,' he snarled.

'Better take it easy, Fallon!' a voice called, and he swung to see Falstaff riding up.

'Fallon?' the wounded towner gasped. 'So you're the one they're all after . . . you're the cause of all this trouble!'

Fallon couldn't make sense of this,

and didn't try. 'Where's the marshal?' was all he wanted to know. No matter how many scum were abroad here today he knew St George to be the real danger both to himself and likely everyone else.

'Go straight to hell — ' the man began but Fallon's backhander chopped him off and had him seeing double with blood leaking from a busted mouth.

'St George — last chance!' Fallon panted, ramming Colt muzzle against teeth.

'G-gone.' This hellraiser was all through.

'Dead?'

'No. He's gone up-valley to that there chapel . . . where they've took the prisoners . . . '

He clawed feebly at Fallon's shirt front, fighting to keep hold onto the material . . . to life itself. Yet it was all slipping away from him, slipping fast. He opened his lips for one last word but had left it too late. With a convulsive shudder he was gone, a thin trickle of crimson running from the corner of his mouth.

For some odd reason Fallon was touched. But he didn't let it show. 'Three less,' he said harshly, hating how cold and callous that sounded. Scanning his Brethren companions, Fallon saw that Lawson was also wounded, like Krebbs. 'Take cover till the fighting's finished,' he commanded them, pointing to a thick copse nearby. Then, turning to Grenville and Falstaff, he ordered, 'Let's dust.'

★ ★ ★

Rising smoke guided the three hard riders unerringly through the woods and tall forests to bring the town into sight.

It was encircled, a sight that caused them to slew their horses to a halt atop a grassy knoll and stare down. They were haggard-faced and breathing hard.

Several buildings were already ablaze and dead and wounded littered the battleground.

'We're getting whupped!' groaned Falstaff, grey around the gills and sweating profusely from the hard ride.

'Maybe not,' declared Fallon.

'Get shook of your blinkers, man!' Falstaff yelled angrily. 'Can't you see? There's a ring of guns around the town and there's no way the people can fight their way out. My sister and brother are down there and they're as good as dead — '

The back of Fallon's hand slammed across the man's cheek, knocking him from his saddle.

'Get a grip on yourself, man!' There was steel in Fallon's voice. He was a man transformed by crisis. Not so long ago he'd arrived home too late to save his own wife from her killer. The notion that something like that could be repeated here was intolerable.

Nothing and nobody would hold him back now, be he Outsider, Brethren or the State militia!

Yet his voice was steady enough when he spoke. 'I don't see any sign of St

George down there yet, which means that dying man was most likely telling the truth. And if St George is up at the High Chapel and separated from his main force, then there's a chance we could get him. Take him out of this fight — and I've a hunch this whole dog pack might just fall apart.'

His voice was hoarse with emotion. Yet his words hit home hard, even with Falstaff. The man straightened, sleeved his bloodied mouth and spoke haltingly yet with conviction.

'Sorry, Fallon . . . won't happen again.' He squared his shoulders and gestured. 'Sounds like a plan that might work . . . and has gotta have a mile better chance than riding down there across open country to get carved up, eh Grenville?'

Head bobbed in grim agreement and Fallon swung his lathered horse about and went storming into the trees. The trio rode north at the gallop.

★ ★ ★

St George swung his arm and slapped Rebecca March across the cheek. Treece moved fast to stop the girl from falling. He held her upright as St George advanced again.

'It's not my habit to mistreat women,' the lawman lied, 'but you're the one he was sweet on so it's odds-on you know where he is holed up, right now! So, again — where is that son of a bitch Fallon?'

Dazed but defiant, Rebecca threw a bitter stare of accusation at Deacon Brown who stood trembling against the chapel wall with a six-gun muzzle jammed into his soft throat. Had the deacon not blabbed to their captors concerning her and Fallon earlier, the marshal wouldn't be beating her up now.

Crack! The blows were getting harder.

Mother March had fainted after Elder Mortimer was gunned down by the Outsiders. Elder March had put up a fight but was out of it now, slumped in a chair nursing a broken arm. Matthew Brown protested as Becky's ill-treatment continued but lacked the courage to intervene. There was a demonic look about St George and it seemed he might not even stop at murder should she fail to tell him where he might find Jack Fallon.

During the bloody battle at the town St George had learned from a wounded member of the Brethren that Fallon was not among the defenders there. Having already heard that a party led by Sheriff Dolan had taken captives up at the High Chapel, the marshal and Treece had immediately set out for the chapel. But all they had found were several dead men and an hysterical group of wedding guests, none of whom either could or would divulge what the marshal wanted most to know — where was Fallon.

St George screwed a fist in the bodice of Rebecca's wedding gown and drew her face close to his own.

'You damned little fool!' he hissed.

'You know the man you're protecting is a tried and convicted woman-killer, don't you? His own wife! Murdered her in cold blood, which is why the bastard's on the run. Yet you're protecting him!'

'I don't believe that . . . I'll never believe it!'

'So . . . you are willing to die and see others die just to protect scum like him?'

'We both know who is the scum, Marshal. And it isn't Jack Fallon.'

St George suddenly produced his Colt and raised it to touch Rebecca's temple. He pulled the trigger. In the shocked silence everybody heard the hammer click on an empty chamber. One of the deacon's wives screamed in shock and terror, but the girl was impassive. St George appeared confounded by her stoic calm.

'You . . . you'd really rather die than tell me where that butcher is,' he hissed disbelievingly. Then understanding hit. 'By Judas — you're in love with him!

You have to be to act so crazy!'

'Yes I am!' she cried defiantly. 'I love Jack Fallon with all my heart and shall until I die. So go ahead and do your worst, Marshal St George!'

Puzzlement and anger battled for supremacy in the lawman's face.

'You . . . you love Fallon . . . yet were prepared to marry this senile old goat?' St George said, indicating the huddled deacon with his .45. 'I don't figure — '

'Oh, Becky!' the deacon chided, at last finding the courage to speak up. 'I knew you cared for Brother Fallon, but I had no idea that — '

'Shut your stupid flapping mouth!' St George snarled, rearing back in rage and disbelief. He sleeved his mouth, fought for control then touched Rebecca's breast with the .45. 'All right . . . enough hoopla. Last chance. Where is that bastard? Tell me or I'll kill you, I swear to God!'

'Shoot and be damned, Marshal!' she hissed in his face.

For a hanging moment St George

seemed locked in indecision, trigger finger still holding first pressure. Then he mastered himself with effort and stepped back. 'Take her outside. I'll shoot her first then go on shooting the rest one by one until somebody talks, I don't give a damn who. Well, move damnit, move!'

It was at that moment as the marshal headed for the doors, that the deacon broke.

'He is gone, Marshal!' he declared. 'Brother Jack Fallon is no longer in this valley. He left last night and we never expect to see him again!'

'Deacon!' Becky chided. 'You shouldn't have spoken. They'll go on hunting him now.'

'I couldn't stand by and see you killed,' Brown protested. 'Even if I know now you don't love me.'

In that moment St George suddenly lost all colour. The power and vitality of the man appeared to seep from that rawboned body as he stood staring from face to face. His dismay at what he'd just heard seemed disproportion- ate to what he'd been told. It was as if he regarded the capture or killing of Jack Fallon as something not only to be desired, but which could be imperative for his own survival.

'Gone from the valley?' He couldn't believe it. He'd put a Herculean effort into this manhunt — for reasons only he understood. Then his expression altered as he rounded on Francine with a soft curse.

'Why the hell should I believe her?' He seized Francine by the hair and brought his Colt up to touch her breast. 'She's lying . . . admit she is, bitch!'

'She's telling the simple truth,' Francine gasped, white with terror. The girl was too scared to lie and even St George could see that. He flung her away from him and rammed the .45 back into leather. Nobody spoke. The man's raging emotion dominated them all.

'Gone . . . ' he muttered. 'All of this . . . for nothing . . . '

'Hardly for nothing, Marshal,' the sheriff tried to console him. He spread his hands. 'Look where we are. We wanted for years to come and clean out these God-botherers and now we got the chance to — '

He broke off as a hard shoulder brushed his chest to send him reeling backwards and St George disappeared through the doorway trailed by the faithful Treece. Dolan hurried out after the pair to see them making for their horses tethered to the chapel fence. 'Marshal, if you're making back for town, hold on, I'm coming with you!'

But Marshal St George was waiting for nobody as he went storming away in a billow of yellow dust. Following at a safe distance, even his own henchmen were puzzled by his reaction. Both had known the marshal over a period of time and so were well aware of his moods and violent tantrums. But his behaviour ever since Fallon had galloped out of San Pedro with a noose flapping free around his neck weeks earlier had caused them to suspect this was more than just a manhunt. It was almost as though the toughest lawman in the county might be actually afraid of Jack Fallon.

But surely that didn't even begin to make sense? St George was afraid of nobody. Wasn't he?

10

The Final Guns

Once well along the trail Fallon, Grenville and Falstaff rode on swiftly and without speaking, cutting away north by northwest along a winding track which took them beyond the maple woods above Canyon Creek. From there they followed the longer but safer route around King John Hill which ensured they would not encounter Outsiders en route, which could have happened had they taken the direct trail.

Fallon's mind raced as he lit up a quirley. Far above he could glimpse towners moving about the High Chapel and motionless figures sprawled in the grass. His jaw muscles worked and he was envisioning the violence that had plainly erupted there. But calming himself with an act of will he began assessing the situation objectively. Due to the number of horses and rigs visible at the chapel it was plain the enemy was still inside and most likely holding hostages. There had as yet been no sighting of either St George or Rebecca March. He refused to decide if this should be seen as encouraging or ominous.

Suddenly Grenville tapped him on the shoulder and pointed east. Two hellions were to be seen heading their way along a game trail, swigging on bottles and plainly oblivious of their proximity in their cluster of elm.

'We'll bail them up,' he ordered, backing his mount deeper into tree shadow.

'But why, Brother Jack?' queried Grenville. 'Wouldn't it be wiser either to gun them down or simply let them go by?'

'Do as I say!' Fallon said harshly. 'But don't shoot unless you have to.'

The Outsiders jerked back in shock

as a trio of armed men suddenly erupted from the trees to surround them. One man threw up both hands but another made a clumsy attempt to use the heavy sawn-off shotgun he carried looped by a rawhide thong slung across his stubby body.

It was only because the man was both drunk and slow that Fallon had time to spur in close and smash him unconscious with his gun barrel before he could bring his cumbersome weapon into play.

He dropped like a stone and Fallon brought his mount up flank-to-flank with the second rider, a big man with fear in his eyes who had no notion what he intended as he rammed his gun in his face. 'Do you know who I am, pilgrim?'

'No-no . . . er, sir.'

'Good. Next question. How many of you scum at the chapel?'

The man was looking more fearful by the minute, so he talked straight. 'Mebbe four or five. We was coming up to . . . to kinda have some fun with the ladyfolks . . . '

His voice trailed off when he sensed he might be saying too much. Fallon held him with an unblinking stare, finally nodded. He reckoned he was hearing the truth; this one was plainly too scared to lie.

Hipping around in the saddle he squinted through the trees at the distant chapel, his mind racing. What he was planning was dangerous but simply had to be done. No other way.

He was peeling off his jacket as he spoke. 'Get me that jacket and hat along with the sawn-off and any ammunition he might have been toting,' he ordered, indicating the unconscious figure on the trail. Although puzzled, his companions jumped down to comply, leaving him to turn back to his shaky hostage.

'You're taking me into the chapel, pilgrim. Act natural or you'll take a double blast from this. Falstaff, you and Grenville wait here for my signal. If you don't get it you'll know I've failed, so you can suit yourselves what you do from there on in. But whatever you do or don't do, I want you to do everything possible to help the hostages should I fail. Can I count on you for that?'

Two heads nodded. Falstaff cleared his throat. 'What if you're recognized despite that big coat and hat?' he asked nervously as he handed Fallon the sawn-off and box of shells.

'The towners don't know me and I've a strong hunch St George isn't there ... we'd have sighted him by now I reckon.'

'But what if he is?' Grenville insisted.

'I'll play that card if it's dealt!' Fallon was through talking; he was acting now. He prodded his hostage in the back with the shotgun. 'All right, ugly, let's travel.'

The two men rode clear of the heavy tree shade then out along the winding down-trail. Soon the men posted outside the chapel were watching them come in but showed no sign of alarm. Fallon was banking heavily on the fact that, because of the Outsiders' numbers in the valley by this time, not everybody could possibly know everyone else.

He reckoned his authentic Outsider's disguise along with his captive would see him accepted as one of themselves for those vital, all-important first moments.

And it did.

The watchers were still unfazed as they allowed him to draw within close range by the hitchrail where he swung to ground holding the shotgun under one arm. 'Brought along this joker on account I'm not sure I swallow his story on just who he is,' he announced in a matter of fact way. He was thus able to reach the nearest man in three long strides before propping and whipping the shotgun out from the folds of his long weather coat.

'All right scum!' he shouted. 'Freeze where you are. I'm Fallon!'

Fallon!

The name froze some but galvanized others into action. A bearded towner let out a strangled curse and jerked six-shooter from holster. Fallon drove a charge of shot into his chest, killing him where he stood. He leapt to one side drawing his pistol as the two Outsiders guarding the small party of hostages by the tankstand started in yelling and made their play.

Desperation lent Fallon a six-gun skill he'd never known he possessed.

He drilled one man through the body and was swinging his smoking cutter towards the other when Matthew Brown leapt upon the man from behind and bore him to the ground.

Fallon was streaking for the chapel door as an ugly man came rushing out. He didn't need to shoot at that close range. Instead he swiped viciously with the barrel to land a blow that sent the hellion staggering ten feet into the chapel wall before crashing onto his face, out to the world.

Without a split second to spare Fallon spun back for the doorway and fanned the hammer of his six-gun as two menacing figures appeared side-by-side — only to tumble together in the dust with howling hot lead ripping them apart.

He was still reloading and staring at the dead through roiling clouds of gunsmoke when another dim figure appeared in the chapel's arched doorway . . . a small, trim figure all in white.

He was still struggling to catch his breath when Becky rushed out and flung her arms about him. The enemy here was no more.

★ ★ ★

Silas Krebbs blinked at Lawson as he worked the lever of his rifle and jacked another shell into the chamber.

'What is it, Brother?' the clansman Krebbs croaked, clutching a bloodied arm.

'I don't believe it,' breathed the rifleman, taking aim. 'It's him, the maverick marshal. And he's riding with just a single man with him!'

'But Brother Jack said that us wounded was just to remain here in hiding until the battle was over, Brother. Not fight.'

'He didn't mean this mongrel,' grated hard jawed Lawson. 'St George is responsible for everything that's happened here, the instigator and the leader. Without him the Outsiders will just be a rabble again. Fallon said so, and right now I can deal the enemy a mortal blow with just one good shot. And by God, I shall!'

The oncoming riders were still some distance away yet travelling swiftly with St George bent on keeping clear of the warring parties whilst hoping to get to pick up Fallon's trail.

Had Brother Lawson waited until his quarry drew closer he might well have dealt them a mortal blow. But the man's nerve was not that good and his marksmanship was even worse.

The bullet meant for St George slammed into Elwood Treece's ribs just below the breast pocket of his hickory shirt. Fighting for breath, the rugged blacksmith found it hard to believe he'd actually been shot while riding away from the fighting. Then he crashed headlong with staring eyes and St George glimpsed the fist-sized hole in his back where the bullet had made its exit.

The marshal twitched and raked viciously with spur as the second shot roared out from the leafy barricade ahead. But he was not in flight. His six-gun glinted in his fist as he drove his mount directly towards the thicket.

Lawson panicked. He sprang from cover to fire repeatedly from the waist but his shooting was wild. By contrast the closer St George got the more accurate his gunmanship, bullet after bullet tearing into Lawson's stocky body and breaking him apart inside.

The wounded Krebbs was attempting to draw his hip gun when St George came storming into the thicket.

He deliberately ran the man over, bowling him along the ground like a bundle of rags. Terrified, Krebbs screamed at the top of his lungs, expecting to be killed.

But the marshal didn't want him dead yet.

Leaping from the saddle he reefed the man into a seated position against a deadfall, dazed and bleeding. He slammed him across the face with his gun barrel then rammed the muzzle into his mouth.

'Fallon,' he panted. 'Where is he?'

By chance, St George had snared one of the few Brethren who knew for certain Fallon had returned. He was also lucky Krebbs was half out of his mind with pain and fear.

He talked and St George listened.

Without even bothering to finish him off, St George sprang back into the saddle. He searched for and quickly found Fallon's tracks right where he expected them to be, then followed them at a reaching gallop.

Riding hands and heels he covered the climbing miles leading to High

Chapel. Upon reaching his objective in swift time only to be forced to take cover in the woods, he squatted on his heels for what seemed an eternity.

His quarry was here; he actually caught a glimpse of Fallon once. But there were others also, how many he could not be sure. Yet although driven by murderous intent as he was, the killer dared not risk crossing that wide open stretch of grassland in defiance of a man like Fallon and however many Brethren supporters he might have over there with him.

So he waited.

Down-valley at Trinity the tide of battle finally swung the Brethren's way. With eyes streaming from the smoke of burning buildings Carver Brown stared wonderingly from a bullet-shattered window as he glimpsed Outsiders suddenly breaking away in panic from their positions to fling aside their weapons and raise hands overhead.

Carver knuckled his eyes. What in hell was going on over there? The smoke impaired visibility badly, yet he eventually identified who it was who'd come right up upon the enemy from the rear, leaving them with no option but surrender.

Then he sighted rifle-toting horsemen with brass badges gleaming on their chests!

'Lawmen?' he breathed. 'Where in hell did they spring from?'

The answer, as all the Brethren were to discover after the assault had totally collapsed, was Jodieville, the county seat. And the men responsible for their arrival here were two young horse hunters from San Pedro County, the sons of Tyball Walsh.

The story behind the brothers' dramatic arrival in Resurrection Valley with a dozen Jodieville citizens and the Chief Marshal after a headlong ride to the valley, was a fascinating one. Yet Carver and Aaron Brown barely had time to listen to it before they were on their way back to High Chapel. Desperate to learn what the situation was up there, they were up and riding before the dust of battle had properly settled. The Chief Marshal and four others rode with them.

* * *

When everyone was ready to travel, Fallon led them away from High Chapel and off down the winding trail.

Rebecca rode by his side. Behind them came three rigs carrying the wounded along with the bewildered wedding guests. Fallon, Grenville and Falstaff were the only able-bodied men in the party yet there seemed no reason to expect trouble on the journey down — ever since the messenger had brought word of the timely arrival down below of the Jodieville law party.

Yet no battle could ever be counted as over until the last bullet was fired.

Fallon was twisting a cigarette into shape with deft fingers, reins looped around the pommel, when without warning Marshal St George exploded from a stand of timber off to his right with a six-shooter in his fist.

Fallon's right hand flew to gunbutt. But he did not draw. St George was already close enough to kill him six times over before he could get clear.

Yet Grenville impulsively jerked up his rifle with a curse and threw it to his shoulder.

Without any change of expression St George blew the man clear out of his saddle, killing him with a single shot to the heart. Brethren watched in horror as the body pitched from the saddle into the dust.

'Born a fool and died one!' St George's face was contorted with triumph and hatred as he closed in on Fallon, the smoking gun in his fist glinting. 'A long chase . . . but we both knew I'd get you in the end.' His face turned to stone. 'All I regret is that so many people had to die because of just one filthy killer!'

Fallon felt oddly detached from it all. He felt he'd played every hand in this deadly game well until this, plainly the climax and last run of the cards. And he thought regretfully, 'All that violence and bloodshed which in these final moments seems such senseless waste with the wrong side triumphant — '

'We both know I'm no killer, St George,' he said woodenly.

'We can all testify to Mr Fallon's character and honesty,' Rebecca put in spiritedly. 'You see, Marshal, we've come to know Jack and have seen what a brave, fine man he really is. No man with his character and strength could possibly have murdered his own wife! That will surely be proven at his trial.'

'Much obliged, Becky,' Fallon said soberly. 'But you are wasting your time. You see, St George doesn't intend to take me back to face trial. He never did. He knows that in a court of law his guilt would likely be exposed . . . all the mistakes he's made. He's going to gun me down and finish the job he botched when he tried to hang me.'

'Lift out your gun and drop it!' St

George ordered. 'Then untie that sawn-off from the cantle.' He waved the gun. 'The rest of you have nothing to fear for the moment. I'll simply return this criminal to San Pedro where the law will deal with him as it sees fit.'

His six-gun flickered. 'The Colt, Fallon!'

Fallon removed the .45 from its holster and tossed it into the dust.

'Now the shotgun!'

It was as Fallon was reaching for the rawhide thongs that the sudden drumbeat of fast-running horses rose from somewhere down trail. He shot a quick glance at St George and felt a wild stab of hope when he realized the killer appeared unconcerned, unaware of his danger.

Was it possible that St George didn't know how events had evolved down-valley — and so expected these incoming riders to be friendlies?

He swallowed painfully, his whole body rigid with a wild and desperate hope. If indeed St George was expecting Outsiders to appear, then surely the odds had just swung his own way. Surely?

'Never mind wasting time,' St George barked, jerking his Colt. 'It won't save your neck — '

He broke off as a bunch of riders on lathered horses burst into sight around a stand of brush below to come storming up the slope towards them.

The lead rider was Carver Brown. He was followed closely by Aaron and five others. Three of the five wore marshals' stars on their chests. The last man was a lean and lanky cattleman from San Pedro who clutched a big shotgun as though he knew how to use it.

Shock struck St George like a thunderbolt. Yet the man recovered in a moment in which he saw the whole situation with vivid clarity and realized he had but one chance of avoiding exposure, trial and execution. Silence Fallon at any cost!

There was naked murder in the killer's eyes as, with the horsemen closing in swiftly, he whipped up his gun muzzle to train on Fallon's chest.

He didn't realize that from Carver Brown's angle as he came spurring upslope, it appeared as if the lawman was lining up to shoot Rebecca.

Carver threw up his Winchester in a fluent motion and squeezed trigger. Considering the fact that he fired from a running horse, it was brilliant shooting. The slug struck St George's shoulder and punched him clean out of the saddle. As he struck ground, Fallon sprang down and kicked the revolver out of his hand. Although hurt, St George leapt up and attacked, but was immediately slammed off his feet as Falstaff charged him down from behind with his horse.

As St George was sent flying, Fallon knew he'd just been saved from certain death. He shook his head and stared wonderingly as the Walsh brothers reined in before him.

'Ed, Zeke!' he gasped. 'What the hell are you doing here?'

Before his young horse-hunting pards

from his home county could respond, the tall man sporting the badge of a chief marshal spoke up in a loud voice laced with authority; 'Marshal St George, otherwise known as Abel Fargo, I'm hereby arresting you on several charges of murder.' He shot a quick glance at Fallon before adding; 'And also for the wilful, wanton slaying of Penny Elizabeth Fallon, late of San Pedro!'

Fallon's gaze jerked away from St George, who appeared to be lapsing into unconsciousness. He could scarce believe what he'd just heard. 'What did you say, Marshal?'

'You heard correctly. I am Chief Marshal Crowley of Jodieville, Mr Fallon.' He swung down and fingered back his Stetson hat. He indicated the Walsh brothers. 'These gentlemen came to visit me just two days ago — and it's lucky for you they did.'

The lawman paused to draw breath, then continued.

'They informed me that they were

both with you hunting wild horses twenty miles from town throughout the entire day when your wife was murdered, but were prevented from coming forward to give evidence on your behalf later by their father, who hates all sheepmen to an obsessive degree.'

Comprehension hit Fallon like a thunderclap. The brothers had always been his only alibi on that evil day, yet when they had failed to show up at his trial he'd guessed at the reason. Their fierce-hating old man! Maybe he should be angry now, yet he wasn't. For this was the truth emerging at last — the testimony that would clear him of his wife's murder.

'We're right sorry, Jack,' said Zeke Walsh. 'But the old man always had us scared stiff as you know and we won't pretend otherwise. The only small way we was able to help you at all back then after they tried you, was by ridin' into town that night after you was sentenced and sawing up the gallows tree.'

'From the transcripts of your arrest

and trial, Mr Fallon,' added the marshal, 'and armed with these gentlemen's sworn testimony I pieced together what happened that day your wife died. Knowing you to be out of town, and being the animal we now know him to be, St George evidently planned his attack upon your wife and after assaulting her, silenced her forever.

'I suspect — and this is largely guesswork yet based on the facts — he knew he had to divert suspicion from himself and so waited for you to return home from the horse hunt when he arrested you and charged you with her death. Of course he made sure you were sentenced to death, and had that penalty been carried out as planned then the truth of your wife's death and your innocence would never have been revealed.'

Fallon shook his head wonderingly. He was dazed. 'There's more,' the chief marshal put in. 'Only days ago I was contacted by Sheriff Simpson in Two Dog Bluff regarding evidence that had surfaced there suggesting the description of St George might well prove him to be a notorious Texan rapist named Fargo. I was following that lead when these two pards of yours arrived with their story. I double-checked the evidence at your trial and discovered your wife had been sexually attacked before her death . . . by her killer . . . by Fargo the wanted rapist, alias St George . . . '

Fallon could scarcely think straight. The truth was ugly yet relieving. He sensed that finally, in this moment, his wife would be truly at rest.

The lawman said, 'When I discovered you had accused the marshal of being the killer at your trial I grew deeply suspicious and wired Texas for more information on this Fargo and realized he and St George were one and the same.' He jabbed a finger at the slumped figure on the ground. 'I dare you to deny my accusation, scum!'

'Lies, all lies!' St George grated, abruptly sitting up straighter, showing he'd just been feigning.

'Texas also informed me that this man had masqueraded as a lawman in the past which obviously gave him the expertise to secure his position in your hometown.' He nodded emphatically. 'Yes, Mr Fallon. I'm quite sure we can present both a strong enough case to secure your full pardon and an apology at the same time. And also have this man duly tried, convicted and hanged — the fate you were so fortunate to survive.'

It was at that moment that St George quit feigning weakness and flicked the wicked little sneak gun from his boot top. Triggering as he sprang erect and leapt towards his horse, he drilled Fallon in the shoulder and killed big Carver Brown with a bullet in the heart.

Rolling in the dust with fire in his shoulder as horses plunged wildly about him and women screamed, Fallon got his six-gun working.

He aimed and fired.

St George couldn't believe he'd been hit, then hit again. Could not believe the total agony that consumed him as he crashed from saddle to ground, staring in bewilderment straight up at the sky until it turned black.

Fallon kept triggering until his gun ran empty and his wife's killer was no more, the echoes of the shots muttering away into the mountains.

Chief Marshal Crowley had drawn his six-gun but had not had the chance to use it. He looked up sharply from the dead man to Fallon. Then he nodded understanding.

'Well,' he said finally, 'that might not have been justice by the book, but justice it surely was . . . '

And somebody whispered 'Amen.'

★   ★   ★

A rooster crowed, flapped its wings and strutted along the fence top in the burgeoning light of morning.

The rooftops of Trinity emerged

slowly from the darkness. Again the rooster sounded but it seemed only Rebecca March was abroad to hear it. She'd not slept all night for reasons she could understand only too well. All that time and still no word from Jack. She drew on robe and slippers to step out onto the porch just as the solitary rider hove into sight over the rim, a broad-shouldered silhouette framed against the new light.

Her heart skipped one full beat with hope, yet she dared not believe it was really Fallon until he turned the horse to come directly across to the house where he stepped down by the olive tree.

Her hand flew to her mouth. She'd not heard from him since he had left three weeks earlier, yet here he was, walking towards her, arms extended.

'Jack!'

He held her close in total silence for a long minute before he began to speak. He had received his full pardon and had sold up the ranch, he revealed.

He'd decided to return here to the valley to stay . . . to fight for her against the deacon if he must . . . to defend and protect her against the whole world if needs be . . . in memory of his wife.

Tears coursed down her face as she related her own news. The terrible events in the valley and the loss of his son had wrought great change in Deacon Brown and reminded him he was an old man. As a result he'd released Rebecca from her enforced agreement to become his third bride and decided he should simply make himself happy with the two wives he already had over whatever time he might have left.

They stood close together in gentle silence as they watched the first sunbeams come streaking across the valley to bathe High Chapel in purest white.